Reckoning at El Dorado

When Buster McCloud is accused of killing Aaron Knight and Salvadora Somoza, he doesn't stay a free man for long. US Marshal Lincoln Hawk wastes no time in dragging the outlaw back to Russell Creek. Once there, McCloud confesses to killing Aaron, but claims he didn't kill the woman.

Lincoln's investigation concludes that Salvadora is still alive, and that she's not the only woman to have gone missing from Russell Creek recently. With all the evidence pointing to the ruthless gold prospector Domingo Villaruel, Lincoln must travel into the very heart of Domingo's empire to uncover the truth. There, in the lawless El Dorado, Lincoln faces the toughest battle of his life as he fights to rescue the innocent and to deliver justice to the guilty.

Reckoning at El Dorado

Scott Connor

A Black Horse Western

ROBERT HALE · LONDON

ISBN 978-0-7198-1691-8

Robert Hale Limited
Clerkenwell House
Clerkenwell Green
London EC1R 0HT

www.halebooks.com

Typeset by
Derek Doyle & Associates, Shaw Heath
Printed and bound in Great Britain by
CPI Antony Rowe, Chippenham and Eastbourne

CHAPTER 1

'Were you just speaking to a US Marshal?' Deputy Murphy Stone asked when Sheriff Bill Caldwell returned to the law office.

Caldwell sneered, although for once Murphy didn't reckon his show of disdain was meant for him.

'Sure,' Caldwell said. He stood at the window to watch the marshal ride out of town. 'Lincoln Hawk said that he just happened to be passing through and he heard about our problem.'

Murphy nodded. 'It'll be useful to have someone like him looking for Buster McCloud, too.'

'It sure won't. I'd have found Buster without his help. Now, no matter who tracks him down, everyone will say that I was in so much trouble a US marshal had to step in.'

Murphy smiled and then headed across the office to stand beside the sheriff.

'Then that's all the more reason to make sure we find him first.' Murphy licked his lips as he warmed to his theme. 'I reckon Buster has holed up on White Ridge. If we search systematically, I reckon we'll find him before the marshal even starts his search.'

Caldwell murmured an exasperated sigh. 'It may look to some as if I need a marshal's help, but I hope the day will never come when I need your help to find an outlaw.'

Murphy's shoulders slumped and he turned away from the window.

'In that case, what do you want me to do today?'

Caldwell rubbed his jaw as he considered and then pointed at the adjoining jailhouse.

'Those two drunkards from the Lucky Horseshoe saloon should have slept it off by now. So throw them out their cell.' Caldwell shoved Murphy forward. 'Then I reckon you need to get to work with that mop.'

Buster McCloud had nowhere left to run.

For the last hour US Marshal Lincoln Hawk had followed him on foot as Buster had tracked along the top of White Ridge. Buster had been looking for a route down, but he'd failed and now he was standing on the edge of a sheer drop of over a hundred feet.

'You've caused a whole heap of trouble,' Lincoln said, stomping to a halt ten paces from Buster. 'Now it's time to give up.'

Buster leaned over the edge and looked around. His sorry shake of the head confirmed that he couldn't climb down and so when he turned back to Lincoln he offered a resigned frown.

'I should have realized I'd never get away from a US marshal, but I guess I should be honoured that Sheriff Caldwell had to call you in.'

'He didn't. I just happened to be passing through and I heard he couldn't find you. I reckon he'll be none too pleased I got to you first.'

Buster laughed. 'Then that's a fitting end for me. Escaped from a man who was looking for me and then caught by a man who wasn't.'

Lincoln nodded and then moved closer. Although Buster was packing a gun, so far he'd shown no inclination to fight back, but after their brief chat Buster might be hoping that he was off-guard and so try a last desperate attempt to escape.

Lincoln halved the distance to Buster, ensuring that no matter which way he ran he'd be able to intercept him while making sure he didn't get too close to the edge.

'Put your hands on your shoulders and move forward real slow. When I handcuff you, don't try anything.'

'I have no quarrel with you.' Buster provided a wan smile. 'But then again, I'm not giving myself up.'

'I'd hoped you wouldn't make this difficult on yourself.' Lincoln edged his jacket aside to expose his holster. 'Sheriff Caldwell says you've killed two people, so I'm taking you back to Russell Creek. It's your choice whether you're still breathing when you get there.'

Buster shrugged. 'I'm facing the noose, so the only control I have left over my life is how and when I stop breathing.'

Buster doubled up to look over the edge and for a moment Lincoln thought he'd plucked up the nerve to jump and end his life on his own terms, but then with a gulp he flinched away from the edge.

'That's not the way out for you.' Lincoln rested his hand beside his holster and gestured with the other hand for Buster to approach. 'I've taken in plenty of desperate outlaws and I can tell you're not like them. I'm sure you have a story to tell and nobody will hear it if you jump.'

'I killed Aaron Knight and that's a fact.' Buster rubbed his bristled jaw. 'But I don't want to die with everyone thinking I'm as bad as they say I am, so know this: I didn't kill the woman.'

Lincoln knew only sketchy details of Buster's crimes and so he limited himself to a neutral comment.

'You can tell me what happened on the way back to town.'

Buster hunched his shoulders, seeming as if he'd now give himself up, but with his confession made he kicked at the ground. Then, with a roar of defiance, he spun on his heels and faced the edge.

He crossed his arms over his chest and leaned forward with his head raised. Lincoln watched in horror as he toppled forward and although he'd decided beforehand that he wouldn't risk himself if Buster tried to jump, he ran towards him.

Buster must have heard him coming as he flinched and that ruined his dignified fall. With his arms waving, he twisted as he toppled over the side and so when Lincoln reached him his feet were still on the ground but his body was almost horizontal.

Lincoln dived and gathered a firm hold of Buster's right ankle. Then, with a frantic scramble, he grabbed a trailing end of his jacket with his other hand.

He yanked Buster backwards, but he couldn't stop him from falling and so he gritted his teeth and held on. A thud sounded that dragged Lincoln's arms forward and then everything stilled.

Lincoln shook himself, realizing with a sigh of relief that he was still holding Buster's leg and jacket. Lincoln was lying sideways a foot from the edge while Buster had come to rest with his legs on the rock and his upper body bent over the edge.

Buster was upside down, but he was still waving his arms as he sought purchase on the rock and so Lincoln tried to edge backwards while dragging Buster with him. He failed to find any leverage on the smooth rock and instead his efforts only made him slip in the other direction, letting him see more of the sheer drop below.

'Stop struggling or we'll both go over,' he said.

The moment he'd said the words Lincoln wondered if they'd been wise as they might encourage Buster to struggle more, but Buster's brush with death appeared to have knocked some sense into him and he stilled.

While still holding Buster's leg, Lincoln walked his other hand along Buster's jacket aiming to reach a shoulder, but Buster gathered his intent and reached out with his right hand.

Buster grabbed Lincoln's arm while Lincoln held his elbow. Then Lincoln pulled back and, despite their awkward positions, in short order he tugged Buster's upper body back over the edge and deposited him on the ground.

Buster sat up while Lincoln shuffled away from him before getting up on to his knees.

Buster frowned. 'I guess I didn't want to end it all now, after all.'

'You can't do nothing to change the fact you've killed a man, but I reckon your desire to live means you want justice for this dead woman.'

Buster shook his head. 'The fact I was too scared to end my own life won't provide that, as I don't know nothing.'

Buster cast a last look over the side. Then, with a resigned sigh, he got to his feet and turned away from the edge.

Completing Lincoln's earlier command, Buster put his hands on his shoulders, walked forward for five paces and then held his hands out with the wrists pressed together. Lincoln moved on to face Buster and he didn't speak again until he'd cuffed him and was leading him away.

'Knowing nothing is a start, as I now know that I can trust you.'

Buster uttered a rueful laugh. 'Not many people have ever said that I'm a man they can trust.'

'Except I can. Back there on the edge, there was a moment when you could have easily made me fall over the side.'

Buster shrugged. 'One man was enough for me.'

CHAPTER 2

'Tell me about the man Buster McCloud killed,' Lincoln said when Sheriff Caldwell returned to the law office after locking Buster up in the jailhouse.

'I'm grateful for what you've done,' Caldwell said, folding his arms, 'but this matter is over now and I've got no further use for you.'

'I understand, but I'm moving on and for my own peace of mind I'd like to know what happened.'

Lincoln offered a benign smile and Caldwell considered him, seeming as if he'd relent, but then he gestured at the paperwork on his desk.

'I've got a whole heap of things to do.'

'So have I, but I can spare the time to hear the details, and perhaps talking about it will make this clearer in your own mind.'

'I'm clear enough.' Caldwell set his hands on his hips, but when Lincoln didn't move, he sighed. 'I guess Deputy Murphy Stone is free. He can answer all your questions.'

Lincoln turned to the corner of the office where Caldwell's deputy was leaning back in a chair with his crossed feet planted on an unlit stove and his head rocked back so he could contemplate the inside of his hat. Both lawmen faced him, but Murphy didn't register that he was being talked about and so Caldwell moved over to him and swept his feet down to the floor with a clatter.

'Hey, I was just getting round to doing it,' Murphy muttered sleepily.

'You won't need to now because you've got a new job.' Caldwell indicated Lincoln. 'Take him out to Aaron Knight's place.'

Murphy rocked his head from side to side as if weighing up which of his outstanding tasks he'd prefer to do before, with a shrug, he accepted the duty. As he sloped off for the door, Lincoln dallied to shoot a narrowed-eyed glare at Caldwell, who returned an amused smile.

Once outside, Murphy maintained a languid stroll to his horse and without comment, mounted up and set off out of town. Lincoln settled in beside him and they rode in silence.

A mile out of town they joined a bend in the creek and trotted along beside the water. After another mile they faced a house that stood on an elevated stretch of land.

'Aaron Knight's place?' Lincoln asked when Murphy stopped.

'Sure,' Murphy said around a yawn and then turned

his horse to head back to town.

'And what happened here?' Lincoln called after him.

Murphy rode on for a few paces before drawing back on the reins with an exasperated grunt. He hunched over in the saddle while shaking his head and then turned his horse to face Lincoln.

'Sheriff Caldwell just told me to take you here. He didn't say nothing about—'

'Deputy Stone, I'm a US marshal,' Lincoln snapped, his irritation finally brimming over. 'I don't have the time to waste on a lawman who is worried he didn't do his job properly or on a lawman who doesn't care about his job.'

As he'd done in the law office, Murphy rocked his head from side to side as he considered which description applied to him. He shrugged.

'I'm not sure I can help you. I don't know what happened here. Sheriff Caldwell dealt with that while I looked after the office.'

'You must have heard some of the details while you were sweeping up.'

Murphy winced, but this insult appeared to get through to him as, with his chin set firmly, he dismounted and headed down to the creek. When Lincoln joined him, he pointed at a stretch of shallow water.

'One evening last week prolonged gunfire was heard out here, so the sheriff came to check it out. He found Aaron Knight lying dead on the edge of the water. He'd been shot in the chest and he was

14

drenched, so Caldwell reckoned he'd been thrown in the water, but had drifted back.'

Lincoln nodded approvingly at Murphy's surprisingly effective summing-up.

'And the woman?'

'She was Salvadora Somoza. The sheriff couldn't find her body, but she wasn't in the house and so he reckoned she'd been killed and thrown in the water, too, but she'd not drifted back.'

'Has her body been found?'

'Nope.'

'Do you agree with Caldwell that she must have been killed?'

Murphy tipped back his hat to scratch his forehead, his eyebrows raised presumably in surprise that someone had asked him for an opinion.

'I don't know all the details like the sheriff does, but there was always something mighty odd about the situation with Salvadora.'

Lincoln waited, but Murphy looked around nervously while gnawing at his bottom lip.

'Go on,' he prompted.

'Salvadora worked at the Lucky Horseshoe saloon. Plenty of women have worked there and most don't last long, so it wasn't surprising when one night she was no longer there, but she'd started living with Aaron Knight. She cooked and cleaned for him, and I guess a whole lot more besides.'

'I can guess. So how does Buster McCloud fit into this?'

'He was just a prospector who had returned to town to lick his wounds after another failed expedition. On the night of the shooting he got into an argument with Aaron in the saloon. Then he went on the run and the rest you know because you found him.'

Lincoln looked up at the house, noting even from a hundred yards away the lop-sided walls and the hole in the roof.

'What did Aaron do for a living?'

'Like Buster, he'd prospected for gold up in the Scorched Land, but he never had any luck, so he settled here to fish.'

'There's a lot of demand for fish in Russell Creek, is there?'

Murphy shrugged. 'He always paid his way without trouble, or else I assume Salvadora wouldn't have been happy to go and live with him.'

'I know nothing about Salvadora or her situation, but I get the feeling she might not have had much of a choice.'

Murphy gulped and with that worrying thought he looked at the shallow water, the creek and then the house, his expression now eager as if he was looking for more ways to be useful.

'Does that answer all your questions?' he asked.

'Sure. You've been useful for a man who was just looking after the office when all this was happening.'

Murphy kicked at the ground. 'The sheriff doesn't trust me to do much.'

'Then I reckon he's not using your talents properly

and I'll be sure to tell him that when I see him again.'

'You're staying?'

Lincoln smiled. 'I thought I might stay a while and see what else I can find out about this missing woman.'

Murphy nodded and turned away, but then he stopped and looked back.

'So you reckon she's still alive?'

'From the hints you've given me about her life, I can imagine she might have taken the opportunity the gunfight afforded her to run away. Until I can prove otherwise, I'll view her as only missing.'

Murphy nodded and continued nodding as he moved away. When he'd mounted up, he rode on back to town at a brisk pace.

Lincoln watched him go and then led his horse up the slope to the house. As it turned out, Murphy's opinion that Salvadora had kept the house tidy for Aaron appeared overstated as the place was in a disgusting state.

Even before he pushed aside the door that was hanging off one hinge, the rancid smell of rotting food and filth invaded Lincoln's nostrils. The smell was so bad, he feared that he might find Salvadora's body inside.

As he paced over the discarded clothing on the floor, he breathed through his mouth, but he found only the residue left by people who didn't care about the conditions in which they lived.

What was more interesting was what he didn't find.

He saw nothing to suggest Aaron was as wealthy as

Murphy thought he was, and he found no women's clothing. By the time he slipped outside, Lincoln had firmed up his opinion that Salvadora was still alive.

Having seen the conditions in the house, he hoped that wherever she'd gone, she would be better off, but that thought didn't cheer him. He walked away deep in thought and so he had reached his horse before he registered that he was being watched.

A gaunt man was standing on the other side of the dilapidated fence watching the house. He was dressed in black and he'd set his feet wide apart with his hands clutched before him.

Lincoln acknowledged him with a nod, but the man didn't react. Lincoln still walked towards him and when he reached the fence he noted that the man held a Bible.

'Joshua Vincent,' the man said, his voice deep and resonating with assurance. 'You'd be Marshal Lincoln Hawk.'

'I am,' Lincoln said, although he didn't think that was a question.

'I gather you brought in Buster McCloud for killing Aaron Knight and now you're interested in the missing woman.'

Lincoln looked aside and picked out Deputy Stone in the distance, so he presumed the deputy had met Joshua and explained his reason for being there.

'I am. So can you help me understand what Aaron and Buster were like?'

Joshua gestured at Lincoln with the Bible.

'You'll find everything you need to know about those men in here.'

'And about the missing woman, too?'

'Of course,' Joshua snapped. He turned on his heel and looked as if he'd walk away, but then he stopped and stood with his shoulders hunched.

'Is there something you want to tell me?' Lincoln asked.

'Yes,' Joshua said after a while. He took a deep breath. 'Salvadora isn't the only woman who's gone missing recently.'

'Who was the other woman?' Lincoln asked. He didn't get an answer, and so he slipped through the fence and walked round Joshua to face him. 'Just tell me.'

'Her name was Chastity.'

'Did she have anything to do with Aaron Knight?' Lincoln waited for an answer, but Joshua only stared at him, so he continued with the questions. 'Did she know Buster McCloud? Did she work at the Lucky Horseshoe saloon? Did she—?'

'I've told you everything that matters. Now you must do what you must do, and I must do what I must do.'

With that, Joshua turned and walked away, heading upriver.

'Did you get rid of him?' Sheriff Caldwell asked when Murphy Stone returned to the law office.

'I answered the marshal's questions,' Murphy said,

'but I reckon he'll be back.'

Caldwell nodded. 'The moment I first saw him I knew he'd overstay his welcome.'

'That's as maybe, but he sounded concerned about Salvadora's fate.'

'We all are, but that matter is over now.' Caldwell moved over to the window, presumably to look out for the marshal. 'For you, though, it's time to get busy.'

Murphy smiled, finding that his brief time spent with the marshal had enthused him.

'What do you want me to do?'

'I want you to finish what you started. The cells aren't clean enough yet. I want you to make them shine so brightly you'd be happy to spend the rest of the day in one.'

Murphy sighed. He reckoned he'd sooner while away his day in a cell than spend his time on the menial tasks the sheriff allocated to him, but he kept that thought to himself. He collected a mop, headed outside to collect water and then sloped into the jail-house.

Buster was the only prisoner and he was sitting on his cot in the corner cell with his legs drawn up to his chin. He watched Murphy swish the mop back and forth with the same bored detachment that Murphy contemplated his work.

The cell floors didn't look particularly unclean and Murphy doubted he was doing anything other than make them wet. The only sure thing was that Caldwell wouldn't approve of his work.

'You enjoy your time with Marshal Hawk?' Buster asked after a while.

'Yeah, he was. . . .' Murphy rested his mop against a bar. 'How did you know I'd been talking with him?'

'I'm the only one in here and I hear some of what goes on in the office, especially when Caldwell raises his voice.'

Murphy frowned. 'He didn't like it that the marshal found you and not him.'

'I'd gathered that.' He shrugged. 'The marshal seemed a decent man.'

'He is and he's looking into what happened to Salvadora. In fact he's not sure she's dead.'

Murphy winced, wondering if he'd revealed too much information, especially when it was more than he'd told Caldwell, but Buster accepted his comment with a smile.

'I hope she's fine, wherever she ends up.'

Murphy noted Buster's level tone, suggesting his revelation hadn't surprised him.

'Do you have any idea what might have happened to her?'

'I was busy trying to escape, so I haven't thought about that much.'

Murphy smiled. 'You have plenty of time to think now.'

Buster returned the smile. 'I guess I do.'

CHAPTER 3

Lincoln returned to town at a brisk trot.

He took a route that avoided passing the law office and headed into the Lucky Horseshoe saloon. It was now mid-afternoon and few customers were inside.

He asked for a coffee and took his mug to a corner table where for the next half hour he watched people come and go. Murphy's comments had given him the feeling that this place would be a centre for trouble in town, but for now, the place was quiet.

Most of the people who were whiling away the afternoon were planning to go prospecting in the Scorched Land to the north. So those on their first expedition were animated while the more seasoned veterans eyed the enthusiastic ones with stoic amusement.

He reckoned his presence would ultimately gather interest and sure enough, he was on his second coffee when the owner, Meredith Zale, made his way over to him.

Meredith sported a wide smile that puffed up his glowing red cheeks and he rubbed his hands with delight when Lincoln signified that he should sit with him.

'I hear that you've sorted out our little problem with Buster McCloud,' he declared, speaking loudly, seemingly for the benefit of the few customers. 'For that the town of Russell Creek is eternally grateful.'

'I'm pleased I could be of service, and it's warming to be thanked by a man who speaks on behalf of the whole town.'

Meredith's smile faltered as he presumably tried to work out if Lincoln was being sarcastic. He dismissed the matter with a shrug and then dragged his chair closer.

'You reckon Buster will get the justice he deserves?'

'Everyone deserves justice, whether that be Buster, Aaron Knight or Salvadora Somoza.'

Meredith had been nodding approvingly, but the last name made him frown.

'She was a popular saloon-girl when she worked for me. Buster should hang for killing Aaron, but he should rot in hell for killing a woman like her.'

'Assuming she's dead. After all, I gather her body hasn't been found.'

Meredith shrugged. 'Buster sure had a temper. He'd have killed her, too.'

Lincoln nodded. 'I'd already heard he was arguing

in here on the night of the shooting.'

Meredith opened his mouth to reply and then closed it. He leaned back in his chair.

'You're asking an awful lot of questions for a man who's just passing through.'

'I never said that I'm just passing through.' Lincoln smiled when Meredith registered his mistake with a gulp. 'And you seem awfully nervous for a man I'm just having a pleasant conversation with.'

Meredith stood up quickly. 'Buster was a nasty piece of work and he killed Aaron. What he did to Salvadora I don't like to think about. That's all I have to say on the matter.'

Lincoln waited until Meredith started backing away and then raised a hand, halting him.

'What do you know about a woman called Chastity? Did she work here, too?'

'What's she got to do with Buster McCloud?'

'That's what I want to know. So start at the beginning and answer my first question: Did Buster argue in here with Aaron on the night of the shooting?'

'Don't answer that!' a strident voice demanded from the doorway.

Lincoln turned his head to find that Sheriff Caldwell had arrived. He hadn't seen anyone pass on a message to him that he was here, and Meredith's relieved smile suggested that it hadn't been him.

'I'm just having a friendly chat with Meredith,' Lincoln said.

Caldwell flashed a glance at Meredith that made

Meredith hurry to the bar. Then he glared down at Lincoln.

'Walk with me,' he said before heading outside.

Lincoln followed him and by the time he slipped outside, Caldwell was already walking slowly down the boardwalk and away from the law office.

'What's the problem?' Lincoln asked when he joined him.

'Like I said earlier, I'm grateful for what you've done, but now that Buster is behind bars I have no further need of your help.'

'Normally I'd agree, but it's looking likely that Buster only killed Aaron and not Salvadora. I'm also wondering if Salvadora is not actually dead.'

'There's no body, so that's possible, but one young woman taking her chance to run away is hardly a matter that should concern you.'

'And again, normally I'd agree, but she might not be the only missing woman.'

Caldwell stopped walking and swung round to face him with his eyes narrowed.

'Who told you about that? It surely wasn't that idiot deputy of mine?'

'That idiot deputy of yours answered my questions with more openness than anyone else has, but it wasn't him. A man called Joshua Vincent sought me out.'

Caldwell winced and glanced away while shaking his head. He sighed and then fixed Lincoln with his icy gaze.

'That's the moment when I stop taking any more of your nonsense,' he muttered. 'This is my town and your investigation ends here.'

'This is your town, but I reckon something bigger than just Buster McCloud shooting up a man is going on here.'

'You do, do you?' Caldwell looked him up and down and sneered. 'You ride into town, hear about a man on the run and then hurry off and find him within hours. That makes you think I need your help to dispense justice, but you're wrong.'

'I'm sure you don't need my help, and if everyone had just answered my questions I'd now be riding away from your town without a care. But everyone I've talked to has been evasive and I want to know why.'

Caldwell shook his head slowly and then edged a half pace closer.

'All right. I'll start with Aaron Knight, as despicable a man as I've ever met. I don't know what deal he did with Meredith to get Salvadora into his house, but I hope she got away safely and I'm sure wherever she ran to, she'll be better off there than with him.'

'I hope so, too.'

'Then there's Joshua Vincent, a man with big convictions and an even bigger interest in the women Meredith employs. Every night he comes into town to berate everyone about their wickedness, except when everyone has gone home he administers to Meredith's saloon-girls in his own special way.'

Lincoln shrugged. 'He might just be praying with them.'

'He might, but they charge him the same rate as everyone else.'

'They might do that, but Joshua sounded concerned about this woman Chastity.'

'Joshua played you along and you reacted just the way he wanted you to.' Caldwell stepped back while shaking his head. 'I assume he didn't tell you Chastity's surname?'

'No.'

'It's Vincent.' Caldwell snorted a laugh when Lincoln raised a surprised eyebrow. 'Chastity is his daughter and like Salvadora, if she's run away I'm sure she'll be better off wherever she ends up rather than having to cope with a man like him.'

Lincoln conceded, with an aggrieved sigh, that Caldwell had a right to be angry.

'He didn't tell me that.'

'You don't know the people here. If you did, you'd know that there's no bigger problem. It's just a matter of a man shooting up another man and two women running away seeking something better.'

'I guess I can see that.' Lincoln spread his hands. 'I'll be moving on.'

'Make sure that you do.'

Caldwell glared at Lincoln, but Lincoln decided to let him have the last word and he turned away. Five minutes later he was riding out of town.

He hadn't completely decided that he would let the

matter end there, so he rode past Aaron Knight's house and considered the scene.

He saw nothing that he hadn't noticed before, but one aspect of the situation still made him uneasy and so he headed upriver, seeking out Joshua's house by following the direction Joshua had taken.

He had moved on for two miles without seeing any sign of it when he noticed that someone was following him. He stopped and when the galloping rider came closer he smiled on recognizing Deputy Murphy Stone.

'You got some news for me?' Lincoln hollered when Murphy reached him.

Murphy scowled. 'No. Sheriff Caldwell reckoned that as I answered your questions so well, I should ride along with you and answer any other questions you might have.'

'I don't have any. I'm leaving.'

'That'll please him.' Murphy considered him. 'And I'm sorry. It was me who told the sheriff you'd be heading back into town.'

'That's no problem.'

'I'm relieved.'

They stood in silence for a while.

'You can ride along with me if you like.' Lincoln winked. 'That way you can make sure I leave and I don't ask anyone else any awkward questions.'

'Caldwell did say something like that.' Murphy offered a thin smile. 'You don't mind?'

'I don't see why I should and you can help me.

Before I leave, I want to talk to Joshua Vincent again.'

Murphy winced. 'Joshua was someone the sheriff didn't want you speaking to again.'

'Noted. Now, where does he live?'

'Caldwell wouldn't want me to tell you, so it'd be best if you just kept riding along upriver.'

Lincoln considered Murphy's firm-jawed expression and then nodded and swung his horse around. Murphy slipped in beside him and they rode on quietly beside the creek for another two miles.

When Lincoln espied Joshua's house ahead, he turned to Murphy.

'Is there anyone else Caldwell doesn't want me to speak to before I leave?'

'Aside from Meredith Zale, I don't think so. He just wants you to leave quietly and quickly.'

Lincoln looked around, noting the long length of White Ridge to the south of the creek and the craggy heights of the Scorched Land to the north.

'I figure riding along beside the creek is the most direct route away from Russell Creek.'

'It is. That way it'll take you a day to move off Caldwell's territory.'

'So is there any route he'd prefer me not to take?'

'He didn't say, but I reckon he wouldn't want you heading north to the Scorched Land. It'll take two days that way.'

'The prospectors who head into Russell Creek all go there, so I presume he doesn't want me to annoy them.'

'I presume.'

They rode along until they reached Joshua's house, by which time Lincoln had considered all the subtle angles he could use to probe Murphy for more information, so he settled for the direct approach.

'Are there any other questions Caldwell would prefer me not to ask you?'

Murphy shrugged. 'I'm only his deputy and he doesn't confide in me.'

'I gathered that, but I've also seen that you're more able than he gives you credit for. You see and hear more than he knows about, and I reckon you have a good idea what's worrying him.'

Murphy took a deep breath. 'He might not want you to ask me about the other missing women.'

'There's more?' Lincoln spluttered, aghast.

'I reckon there might be. The saloon-girls in the Lucky Horseshoe saloon don't last there for long, but nobody ever seems to worry about it.'

'Do you know any names?'

Murphy lowered his head. 'I was friendly with this one woman, Mary. She said she had a hankering to head north and go prospecting. She tried to persuade me to go with her, but I didn't want to leave town and then one day she'd gone.'

'You think she found a prospector who was prepared to take her with him?'

'It's possible, and maybe others have done that, too, but it's hard to believe every one of them decided to go prospecting.' Murphy pointed, signifying that

Joshua was coming out of his house. 'Chastity could well have gone north, though. She often chatted with the men who were heading to the Scorched Land and her father didn't approve of that.'

Lincoln didn't reply as he watched Joshua approach. As he'd done at Aaron's house, Joshua stopped by the fence and stood with his legs spread wide apart and his Bible clutched before him.

Lincoln dismounted and stood on the other side of the fence.

'You didn't tell me that the missing woman was your daughter,' he said.

'The moment she left,' Joshua declared, 'she stopped being a daughter of mine.'

'Except you cared enough to seek me out and tell me about it.'

'I thought a lawman might find out where she'd gone.' Joshua inclined his head slightly, which Lincoln took to mean that he wanted to know what he'd found out.

'It seems other women have gone missing besides your daughter and Salvadora Somoza. The most likely place they went is to the Scorched Land and so I'm heading that way.' He glanced over his shoulder at Murphy. 'Sheriff Caldwell's deputy is accompanying me and I hope we'll find some answers.'

Joshua bunched his jaw as he looked past Lincoln to the distant Scorched Land. Then he nodded, as if he'd made a decision.

'I'll join you.'

'I'm pleased. With your help, we might be able to find your daughter and bring her back.'

Joshua shook his head. 'I don't intend to bring her back. If I find her, I'll kill her.'

CHAPTER 4

'Do you believe Joshua's threat?' Murphy asked after they'd been riding along for an hour.

'As Caldwell kept reminding me, I don't know these people,' Lincoln said. 'So do you reckon Joshua is as uncompromising as the sheriff seems to think he is?'

Murphy glanced over his shoulder at the trailing rider and then shrugged.

'I've never had no reason to speak to him before, and I never saw him harass the women in the Lucky Horseshoe saloon. In fact, I reckon they enjoyed talking to him.'

'You gathered that from your friend, Mary?'

'I did.' Murphy considered him. 'She really was my friend and she didn't do what you think she did. She was a bartender, nothing more.'

'I'm not making no judgements on anyone. I'm just heading north in the hope that I can find a missing woman, and hopefully that'll help me work out if other women have gone missing, too.'

Murphy sighed. 'All these disappearances have to be connected, don't they?'

'They don't. The women and their circumstances are all different. Salvadora was a saloon-girl who ended up living with Aaron Knight, while Mary tended bar and Chastity dallied with passing prospectors.'

'Except there's a connection with the Lucky Horseshoe saloon. Joshua and Chastity stood outside the saloon berating people as they went in about the evils of liquor, and then berating them when they left about the evils of looking for gold. Except his daughter wasn't as enthusiastic about the message as he was.'

Lincoln nodded. 'Maybe if Caldwell hadn't stopped me from talking to Meredith Zale I'd have learned if his saloon was important, but luckily from now on I can investigate in places where Caldwell can't intervene.'

Lincoln gave Murphy a long look, making Murphy frown.

'My orders are to make sure you leave. Beyond that, I won't stop you questioning anyone and I won't tell Caldwell what you've done.'

Lincoln smiled, accepting he was unlikely to get any trouble from Murphy, which he couldn't say about his other companion. He slowed to ensure that Joshua rode with them, but he didn't acknowledge them and stared straight ahead.

'You got any ideas where I should start looking?' Lincoln asked.

'The prospectors never listened to my message,'

Joshua said after riding along in silence for a while. 'They would have chosen the wrong path.'

'And your daughter?' He waited, but Joshua didn't reply. 'Were there any prospectors Chastity was especially friendly with?'

Joshua sneered. 'They were all the same, godless and heading for Hell's Gate.'

After Joshua's longest speech since they'd left Russell Creek, he set his jaw firm. Then, with a crack of the reins, he hurried his horse on to take the lead.

'So I guess he doesn't know anything either,' Murphy said, making Lincoln smile.

'Except for the direction I have to take,' Lincoln said. 'It seems I'll have to follow the prospectors to the very gates of hell.'

With that thought they rode on quietly for the rest of the day. Even when they made camp that night and sat around a roaring fire, Joshua didn't join them in conversation, preferring to sit on his own and read his Bible.

His sombre attitude appeared to affect Murphy as he withdrew into himself. So when they rode on the next day, aside from the occasional brief word to discuss the route ahead, the journey was silent.

The higher ground that they were heading towards appeared no nearer than it had done in Russell Creek, making Lincoln revise his opinion on when he could begin his search in earnest.

He figured he wouldn't come across people for several days and so he had settled into the dull routine of the long journey when he saw movement ahead. He narrowed his eyes and discerned that two riders were coming towards them.

The riders were a half mile ahead and the same distance to their left. They were moving on a course that skirted along the base of a higher stretch of land, adopting a route that would pass by them.

Lincoln got his companions' attention and then pointed, making Murphy smile at this change in routine while Joshua didn't react. They were riding on open ground and the moment they set off towards the newcomers it became apparent that the riders had spotted them first, as they stopped and swung round to face them.

The men adopted defensive postures with the high ground at their backs while spreading apart so they could flee in either direction.

Lincoln saw nothing wrong with these men being cautious. They were heading back from the Scorched Land, so they were prospectors and they had probably been lucky.

'You men have nothing to fear,' Lincoln shouted when they were still fifty yards away. 'I just want to ask you a few questions.'

He had barely finished his encouraging words when the men turned away and scooted back along the route they'd taken.

'Perhaps you should have mentioned that we were lawmen,' Murphy said.

'If I had, they're so spooked, they'd have probably

started shooting.' Lincoln speeded up. 'Come on. Let's find out what's worried them.'

By the time they reached the spot where the men had stopped, the riders were galloping around the end of the rise to disappear from view. With Lincoln leading they followed.

Murphy tucked in behind him and Joshua adopted a steadier pace that ensured that he soon fell behind. When they swung around the end of the rise, they faced the entrance to a gulch.

High ground was on either side and the men were no longer visible, so they were forced to adopt a cautious pace. Lincoln and Murphy spread apart to take either side of the entrance, and even though Lincoln peered along the low ground and then up either side, he couldn't see where they had gone.

As the end of the gulch was steep, he would be able to see them if they tried to leave using a route other than the entrance. So he stopped and gestured to Murphy that they should get under cover and wait them out.

Murphy signified a tangle of boulders twenty yards ahead and then set off for them, leaving Lincoln to cross over the gulch towards him. He had reached the halfway point when gunfire erupted, forcing him to speed up.

Without mishap he joined Murphy at a gallop and both men jumped down off their horses. Then, with their heads down, they moved on to the boulder furthest out into the gulch. There, they hunkered down and looked up at the higher ground, but the men still didn't betray their location.

A tense few minutes passed, and when Lincoln saw the first movement it came from Joshua riding through the entrance. Lincoln gestured, urging him to seek cover, but Joshua continued riding along at the same slow pace.

In exasperation Lincoln beckoned him on, but another burst of gunfire tore out, the reports and their echoes rattling away on either side. He stayed close to the boulder, only raising his head when the gunfire died out, but again he could see no gun smoke, or rising dust that might indicate where the shooters were hiding.

'This sure is frustrating,' Murphy said while shaking his head. 'I can't even work out which side of the gulch they're on.'

'We might get a chance,' Lincoln said, 'if Joshua carries on giving them something to aim at.'

He gestured again at Joshua, who drew his horse to a halt. Then he leaned forward in the saddle as if contemplating the fact that there was no route available out of the gulch rather than that he was avoiding the gunfire.

Then, with a wince, Lincoln acknowledged that Joshua might not be acting as foolishly as he'd first thought. Testing a theory, he raised his head and when that didn't encourage gunfire, he stood up.

Murphy backed his theory and he joined him in standing up. Then the two men moved into the open and turned on the spot.

'If we weren't the targets, was it those riders?' Murphy said when a minute had passed without reprisals.

Lincoln shrugged and then they moved on down the gulch on foot. They walked sideways with their backs to each other so they could cover each other, letting Lincoln see that Joshua was looking up the gulch on his side.

He got Murphy's attention and a few moments later Murphy pointed out a clearing ahead. Lincoln saw shadows moving that were large enough to be the men's horses, an observation he confirmed when the full extent of the clearing came into sight.

As the horses were alone, he directed Murphy to stay in the clearing and then made his way up the side of the gulch. He moved quickly, now sure that he'd previously misunderstood the situation.

Sure enough, when he saw the two men, they weren't moving. One man had a blooded chest and was lying on his back and the other man was sprawled over a boulder face down with his arms dangling.

Lincoln sighed, noting that finding gold was only half the battle for prospectors. They then had to protect whatever they'd found.

He looked around for their shooters, noting that the rim of the gulch afforded a good view of their position. He gestured down at Murphy and then at the higher ground, and the deputy showed he'd understood his order when he aimed at the top of the gulch.

Lincoln moved on, clambering up to the rim without incident, and then hurried over the flat top with his head down. When lower terrain came into view, he saw movement, but it was of dust rising from riders beating a hasty retreat.

They were already some distance away and Lincoln couldn't discern how many were fleeing, but he judged that there were at least six of them. He shrugged in surprise that they hadn't stayed, as they hadn't had enough time to get to the prospectors' belongings and with their superior numbers they should have expected to prevail against Lincoln and Murphy.

When he'd dragged the two men back down into the gulch, Murphy confirmed that the men's belongings appeared intact. Even stranger, he couldn't find any gold in their saddlebags. The only items they had that were worth stealing were their surprisingly bulky supplies.

'So they're loaded down with the tools you'd expect prospectors to have,' Lincoln said, summing up the situation, 'and they were heading back from the Scorched Land. They had no gold, but they did have supplies.'

'So they must have given up searching quickly,' Murphy said. 'As someone followed them and killed them, I'd guess they made enemies.'

'I'd guess that, too.' Lincoln gave Murphy an approving slap on the shoulder and then turned to Joshua, who had ridden into the clearing but had stayed on his horse to watch them. 'I'd be obliged if you'd help me find somewhere to bury these men.'

Joshua snorted. 'That won't help them now. They sought to enter hell, and that's what they got.'

Murphy broke off from rummaging through the saddlebags to give Joshua a bemused look and then turned to Lincoln.

'I'll help you, but what do we do then?' he said. 'Find out where the dead men came from, or go after their killers?'

Lincoln smiled, noting how this incident had changed his view on both his companions.

For all his sullen brooding and righteous pronouncements, Joshua had understood this situation quicker than he had. For his part, Murphy had proved he was more astute and proficient than he'd expected from a man who Sheriff Caldwell only trusted to sweep out the law office.

'The killers know this area better than we do and we'll struggle to track them down,' Lincoln said. 'So we'll follow the prospectors' trail back to where they came from and find out what they did to get shot up.'

CHAPTER 5

It was mid-afternoon when Lincoln found the last place that the prospectors had visited.

He had followed their trail to a trading post where a sign outside proclaimed that it was the last place to stock up on supplies before El Dorado. Murphy and Joshua hadn't been aware this place existed and the remoteness of the location ensured that the owner, Yancy Wenlock, charged excessively for his few commodities.

Joshua had ensured they had enough supplies for several weeks, so Lincoln left the other two outside and headed in. He considered the paltry produce on offer before opting to buy coffee. He counted out five dollars on to the counter, but when Yancy moved for the money, Lincoln slapped a hand on his wrist.

'This is twice the amount I'd expect to pay,' he said.

'Then go to Russell Creek and buy it there,' Yancy said with studied boredom, as if he'd expected this response.

'I've been to Russell Creek, and I find it interesting that nobody there mentioned you. Perhaps if more people knew you existed you wouldn't have to charge so much.'

Yancy's gaze flicked up to consider Lincoln's star.

'Perhaps, but I like things just the way they are.'

Lincoln glanced around the small room. 'I'm surprised you earn enough to survive when even the few customers you do get end up dead.'

Yancy flinched and offered a surprised expression. His reaction looked genuine to Lincoln, and so removed his belief that Yancy may have helped the prospectors' attackers.

'Who died?' he asked.

'I hoped you'd tell me. Two prospectors were bushwhacked a half day from here on their way back to Russell Creek.'

Yancy winced and then looked at Lincoln's hand until Lincoln relaxed his grip. Yancy moved away and walked back and forth behind the counter as he chose his next words carefully.

'I don't know who they were. Like everyone who has been in the Scorched Land they'd heard about me. It was their first prospecting mission and it hadn't gone well. So they wanted liquor, and for someone to lend a sympathetic ear and offer some encouragement.'

'Did you?'

'No. I told them the truth that it'd only get worse. So they left.'

'Could the reason they lost heart be down to seeing

43

some trouble up there?'

Yancy shrugged. 'They might have made enemies. Then again, many of them face trouble and get followed when they leave.'

'You clearly know plenty about the people who go to and from the Scorched Land.' Lincoln waited until Yancy murmured an affirmative grunt. 'I'm looking for a woman who headed that way.'

'I don't know nothing about no woman,' Yancy said quickly.

'There could be more than one woman who—'

'I said I don't know nothing.'

Lincoln nodded and glanced at the money, seemingly confirming that he'd heard enough and so Yancy slipped it under the counter. Then, while smiling pleasantly, Lincoln signified that Yancy should join him in heading to the door where he pointed at Murphy and Joshua.

'These men are my travelling companions. The young man is no trouble, but the gaunt man is looking for his daughter. He's determined to get answers.'

'Then I'm sorry for him that I can't give him any.'

'And I'm sorry for you that you can't. You see, I'm a lawman and I have a sense of duty, but that man doesn't and if I tell him you're a man with information, he'll sure—'

'I can't help you,' Yancy snapped. 'I'm a trader, nothing more. I sell liquor and beans to people passing by and I sure wouldn't get involved in selling women.'

Yancy gulped, clearly knowing he'd made a mistake the moment he'd said the words, but Lincoln took his time in replying as if he were digesting this information.

'I find it interesting,' he said, speaking slowly, 'that even though I only said I was looking for a woman, you assumed I was asking about women who had been sold.'

'I don't know nothing,' Yancy said with a resigned tone.

Lincoln didn't keep Yancy waiting for his inevitable reaction. He grabbed his collar, marched him across the room, and slammed him up against the counter.

'Talk.'

'I can't,' Yancy whined.

'I can work out what goes on here when you're not selling liquor and beans. You keep quiet about your operation because your customers like it that way. They have things to sell and you don't ask how they got them. I don't care about that. All I care about is the missing women.'

Yancy lowered his gaze and gulped. When he spoke his voice was barely audible.

'Domingo Villaruel, that's all you're getting.'

'Who is he?' Lincoln waited, but Yancy didn't reply. 'Where is he? What does—'

'You need to listen. That's all you're getting, and that's all your gaunt friend outside will get out of me, too.'

'Will I find him in El Dorado?' Lincoln persisted.

'El Dorado isn't a real place. It's the name the prospectors give to the end of their journey where they hope they'll strike it lucky.' Yancy snorted a laugh. 'For most, it's just a myth.'

Yancy fixed Lincoln with a narrow-eyed glare and this time Lincoln relented.

'Obliged. You've been most helpful. When I catch up with Domingo Villaruel, I'll be sure to tell him who pointed me to him.'

Yancy shrugged, this threat not showing any sign of worrying him into revealing more. So Lincoln left him and headed outside.

'You were in there for a while,' Murphy said.

'Yeah,' Lincoln said.

Murphy gave him an odd look, but Lincoln decided to keep what he'd learned to himself. He didn't want Joshua to know what Yancy had said before he'd worked out in his own mind whether he thought this investigation was about to take a dark direction.

With the post being popular Lincoln couldn't distinguish the tracks the prospectors had made before they had arrived there and so he settled for heading north.

He was no nearer to reaching an answer to his problem when they arrived at a brackish creek and settled down for the night. As usual Joshua sat apart from them, while Murphy appeared to have concerns of his own as he looked at the water, then at the higher ground ahead and then back towards Russell Creek.

'I have a decision to make,' Murphy said when

46

Lincoln sat beside him.

'If it helps,' Lincoln said, 'Yancy didn't appear to know anything about the men who shot up the prospectors, so I'm not sure we'll come across them again.'

'That's not what's on my mind.' Murphy pointed at the water. 'This creek marks the edge of Sheriff Caldwell's territory. His orders were to make sure you left, and so once you cross over the water tomorrow, you'll have done that.'

'Then tonight you need to think about what Caldwell would want you to do.'

Murphy nodded. 'And then do the opposite?'

Lincoln laughed and although he saw the hopeful look in Murphy's eyes that said he wanted him to make the decision for him, he didn't offer encouragement, figuring he needed to work this through on his own. Instead, he used what could be his last opportunity to see if Murphy knew more than he'd revealed so far.

'Back in the trading post, Yancy said I needed to look for a man called Domingo Villaruel. Do you—'

Lincoln broke off when Murphy flinched, his shocked expression providing its own answer.

'I know Domingo.' Murphy picked up a stone and hurled it into the water. 'He was the reason I became a deputy lawman in the first place.'

'So it's likely Domingo could be behind whatever trouble is happening out here?'

Murphy gathered up another stone and hefted it

before launching it, this time throwing it beyond the water to land in the dirt on the other side.

'It's likely. Six months ago I was tending bar in the Lucky Horseshoe saloon when Domingo rode into Russell Creek. He claimed he was another prospector looking for El Dorado, but a customer heard strange noises coming from the back of his wagon. I investigated and I found a woman. She was distressed and she'd been beaten. I reported it to Sheriff Caldwell. He said I'd done the right thing.'

'Did Caldwell do the right thing?'

'The woman wouldn't level any accusations against Domingo, but she didn't want to be with him. So the sheriff did the only thing he could do and ran him out of town. He deputized me to stay with Domingo and make sure he left. I did such a good job, I stayed on with him.'

Lincoln snorted a brief laugh. 'It sounds like you're good at escorting. Who was the woman?'

Murphy threw another stone into the water.

'She was Salvadora Somoza, the woman you're looking for.'

Lincoln winced. 'Then the way it's looking, Domingo could have returned secretly to kidnap Salvadora and he might have spirited away Mary and perhaps Chastity, too.'

'I hope not. Salvadora would never talk about her experiences with Domingo, but I could tell they were bad.'

Murphy gulped, his earnest gaze showing he hoped

Lincoln would refute the worrying thoughts that were clearly on his mind, but his information had ensured Lincoln couldn't do that.

'Then we need to find Salvadora, and quickly.'

Murphy nodded until he registered Lincoln's exact words.

'You're telling me that I should stay with you?'

'Nope.' Lincoln waited until Murphy frowned, and then leaned towards him. 'I could appoint you as a special deputy, but I reckon in this case I need all the help I can get. Return to town and tell Caldwell what we've found out about Domingo and the missing women.'

Murphy looked at the creek while biting his bottom lip, and then turned back to him.

'He'll be concerned, but as you pieced together this information, I'm not sure he'll do anything.'

'Then you need to make sure that he does.' When Murphy looked doubtful and moved to pick up another stone, Lincoln slapped a hand on his arm and looked at him sternly. 'You're a good man with good ideas, but you're not letting Caldwell see what I've seen in you.'

Murphy sighed. 'I'll do my best.'

Lincoln gripped his hand more tightly and winked.

'Just follow your instincts and you'll be fine.'

With that, Murphy smiled and moved away to sit beside the fire.

That night, as they ate and rested up, Lincoln noted that Murphy appeared more confident than he'd been at any time since he'd met him. He even spoke with Joshua and tried to find out if he knew anything else that he could report to Caldwell.

The next morning Lincoln didn't burden Murphy with any more advice, trusting that he'd said enough already. So with the minimum of fuss and conversation Murphy left them while he and Joshua crossed over the creek.

A few hundred yards on, Lincoln glanced over his shoulder to check that Murphy was heading back to town. Then he concentrated on the next stage of the journey.

His sullen companion didn't offer any suggestions as to where the prospectors usually headed beyond his standard answer that they were heading into the gates of hell. So Lincoln reckoned they had no choice but to move on and hope to come across tracks they could follow to people who could answer his questions.

Lincoln held out no hopes that this would be a quick process, but late in the day he found the tracks of two riders. With the Scorched Land attracting many visitors, the odds were against these men being connected to the men who had been ambushed, but finding a trail to follow heartened him.

When they drew up for the night, the small amount of progress even made Joshua more animated, although as usual, he ignored Lincoln and took solace in reading his Bible. The next day they followed the tracks into a winding pass that stretched on for several miles until the pass opened up to face a rock cliff that towered above them on all sides.

Lincoln struggled to see where they could go next other than to just turn around and head back down the pass, but thankfully as they approached the base he saw signs of industry.

Thin streams of water cascaded down from above. Where the water came together to form a channel that flowed away down the pass, a wooden contraption had been built.

Lincoln figured it had been built to divert water and then sluice dirt, and it appeared well constructed, but it had been abandoned, as had the small camp beyond. He got within fifty yards of the camp before he discovered the reason why.

Two bodies lay beside the blackened remnants of a fire.

CHAPTER 6

At a fast trot Deputy Murphy Stone rode into Russell Creek.

Although he had dreaded talking with Sheriff Caldwell, he was now eager to complete what was sure to be an uncomfortable meeting.

He had made good time, returning to town a half day faster than he and the marshal had left it, but he still reckoned he'd been away for longer than the sheriff expected. Sure enough, the moment he dismounted outside the law office, Caldwell came hurtling outside to consider him with irritation.

'Where have you been?' he demanded.

Murphy said nothing until he'd headed inside.

'I did what you told me to do and made sure that the marshal left,' he said when Caldwell followed him in. 'The moment he left your territory, I returned.'

Caldwell's mouth fell open in a show of surprise.

'I know I have to carefully spell out instructions to

you, but I never expected you'd stay with him for days.'

'I had to. The marshal uncovered incriminating evidence and so I had to help—'

'I told you to stay with him so he wouldn't do any more uncovering. I certainly didn't want you to help him make a fool of me.'

'That's not what he was trying to do. He thinks Salvadora Somoza is still alive and that she and several other women have been abducted and taken north to the Scorched Land.'

'Then he's wasted his time. That's not happening.'

'Except he came across the name "Domingo Villaruel". It seems that when you ran him out of town he didn't go far.'

Caldwell had raised a finger, seemingly preparing to chastise him again, but the mention of Domingo's name made him soften his expression and concede Murphy's concern with a nod.

'That's one name I never wanted to hear again. I won't complain if the marshal makes his life a misery.'

Murphy sighed with relief. 'Lincoln will need plenty of help to find him.'

'If Domingo returns to Russell Creek, I'll deal with him, otherwise the marshal won't get any help from me.'

'Domingo's a tough critter. If you're not prepared to go after him, I'd sure like to.'

'You're not doing nothing other than what I tell you to do.' Caldwell rubbed his hands. 'And now you're back I have an important task for you.'

Murphy considered Caldwell's sneering expression, something he had directed at him many times before, and then sighed again, this time in exasperation.

'The marshal reckons I could do more than just mop out the cells and sweep the office. He found my help useful and he said I should use my initiative more.'

'He's right.' Caldwell waited until Murphy smiled hopefully. 'So tonight, after you've cleaned up the office, you can guard the prisoner. I reckon I'll enjoy a night in the Lucky Horseshoe saloon.'

Murphy's shoulders slumped. He shuffled a boot through the dust as he tried to recall the arguments he'd rehearsed to talk Caldwell round, but the points he could remember no longer felt as if they'd work.

He offered no more complaints and so, with Murphy having accepted his orders, Caldwell relented from his stern approach and let him leave the office for an hour to get something to eat.

As it turned out, a meal didn't cheer him and as he sloped back to the law office he couldn't help but feel like a failure. The marshal had trusted him with an important task and he couldn't think of a way to overcome Caldwell's reluctance to act.

That gloomy thought brought to mind the marshal's last instructions that he should follow his instincts, and that made him glance across the main drag. Aside from Domingo Villaruel, the other connection to the trouble appeared to be the Lucky

Horseshoe saloon, and so, at a determined pace, he headed there.

He had spoken to Mary most often and so he sought out Jeanette, a saloon-girl who had been Mary's friend. He bought her a drink and chatted about inconsequential matters to give him time to think what questions Marshal Hawk would ask.

'Have you heard anything about Mary recently?' he asked after a while.

'I haven't,' Jeanette said with a shrug.

Murphy nodded. 'It seems the girls working here often don't stay for long.'

Jeanette considered him oddly, clearly having noticed his weak attempt to ask his question in a casual manner.

'Are you leading on to asking me about Salvadora Somoza?'

'How did you know that?'

'Because I'm used to talking and I know when men want something.' She laughed. 'You're more obvious than most.'

'I guess I am. Were you here on the night Buster McCloud argued with Aaron Knight?'

'I wasn't.'

Jeanette looked around, presumably hoping that someone would come over and curtail their conversation, but it was late afternoon and few customers were there, so she failed to catch anyone's eye.

'So that means you don't know anything about Salvadora either?' Murphy waited, but she continued to look around. 'Or Domingo Villaruel?'

She flinched and swirled round to face him, her mouth opening to offer a sharp retort, but then she thought better of making it and downed her whiskey instead. With a determined flounce she turned away and so Murphy lunged forward and grabbed her arm, halting her.

His action ensured that he achieved what she'd failed to do in drawing attention to them.

'Leave me alone,' she said with quiet menace. 'Or even a lawman will walk out of here with more than a few bruises.'

'I'm glad you have some fight in you. Make sure you remember that attitude if Domingo comes for you.'

'Now that Aaron is dead, I doubt that'll happen.'

The moment she'd snapped back her retort she winced, demonstrating that while angry she'd revealed more than she'd wanted to.

'So Domingo was a friend of Aaron Knight?' He waited, but she said nothing and so he opened his hand.

'I'm not answering your questions,' she said before turning away.

'You already have,' he called after her, making her halt for a moment. Then she casually moved on to a corner table where she struck up a jovial conversation with two customers.

Several men were still looking at Murphy, and so he left the saloon. When he resumed his journey to the law office, he did so in a more contented frame of mind.

Caldwell showed that he'd noticed his alertness by not pouring scorn on him while he relayed his instructions for the evening. When he left him, Murphy made himself a coffee and settled down at his desk to think through what he'd just learned.

By the time he'd finished his drink he was clear in his own mind what he thought had happened and so he headed into the jailhouse.

'I'd heard that you'd returned,' Buster said, sitting up on his cot.

'I've spent the last few days with Marshal Hawk,' Murphy said without preamble. 'Before I left, you said you'd think some more about what you knew about Salvadora Somoza's fate.'

Buster shrugged. 'I haven't got much else to think about in here, but thinking don't make things any clearer. Does the marshal reckon he can find her?'

'He does, and we've pieced together what we reckon happened.' Murphy moved over to stand before the bars. 'You were worried that Aaron would pass Salvadora on to Domingo Villaruel and so you argued with him in the saloon. Later that night you killed him.'

Buster got up off his cot to face Murphy through the bars.

'You were right about the last part, but I don't know how you think Domingo fits into this.'

Buster's surprised expression looked honest and in a moment it destroyed Murphy's confidence. He moved backwards to sit on the bench that stood against the wall where he lowered his head to contemplate the floor.

'I felt sure I'd figured it out,' he said, mainly to himself before looking up at Buster. 'But if you didn't argue with Aaron about Salvadora, what did you argue about?'

'It was about Letisha, a woman who went to stay with him, apparently.'

'I didn't know about that.'

'Few people do, and few people seem to care.'

'I care.'

Buster snorted a rueful laugh and then moved back to sit on his cot where he adopted Murphy's posture of leaning forward.

'I first passed through here on the way to the Scorched Land about five months ago.' Buster rubbed his chin. 'I met this saloon-girl, Letisha, in the Lucky Horseshoe saloon.'

'I don't remember her.' Murphy bit his lip, accepting that the direction this story was heading meant she probably hadn't been in the saloon for long.

'I sure remember her. I promised her if I got rich, I'd come back and whisk her away to a better life. She sounded eager, but then again I guess I wasn't the only one who'd made that foolish promise.'

'I assume you didn't get rich?'

'Nope. I found enough to survive out there, but then things took a turn for the worse. There was this secret place deep in the Scorched Land where you could go to trade what you'd found, no questions asked. The rates were poor, but the options were few.'

Murphy leaned forward. 'That would be El Dorado?'

'That's what they called it.'

Murphy whistled under his breath. 'Then it's not just a mythical place.'

'It's not. The place was lawless, but it had rules. Then Domingo Villaruel arrived and it all went bad. I decided to quit while I was still alive and I returned to Russell Creek.'

'And Letisha had gone?'

Buster nodded. 'I asked about her and someone said she'd gone to live with Aaron Knight. I confronted him and he denied knowing her, but I didn't believe him. I followed him back to his house and found this other woman there. Then he got even more argumentative.'

'So you shot him?'

Buster frowned. 'I'd been used to surviving in places like El Dorado, so perhaps I was a mite trigger-happy. What I did wouldn't have raised an eyebrow there, but that's not the way back here.'

'It's not, but I reckon you might still have been justified.'

Buster leaned forward. 'Why?'

'I reckon women got moved on from the Lucky Horseshoe saloon to Aaron Knight. Then Aaron spirited them away to Domingo Villaruel. Letisha was one of those unfortunates, as was a woman I knew, Mary, along with Salvadora, Chastity and perhaps others.'

'Then by shooting up Aaron I may have struck a blow against this operation?'

'Hopefully you dealt the trade a major blow, but it'll need more work to end it.'

Buster nodded, but then frowned. 'The big problem with this explanation is that I've been to El Dorado and I saw no sign of what you think has been going on.'

Murphy shrugged. 'On the other hand, it sounds as if you didn't stay there for long and you weren't looking out for anyone's wellbeing but your own.'

'I guess you could be right. So what are you going to do about this?'

'I need to help Marshal Hawk find Domingo, so you need to tell me how I can find El Dorado.'

'The town is famed for its secrecy, and it's known only to prospectors. Unless you know the terrain you could roam around for months without coming across it and then find you'd passed within a few hundred yards of it several times.'

'I accept that, but if Aaron helped Domingo kidnap Letisha, helping me could help you.'

'It could, but you need to listen to me. You may be following the marshal's advice and using your initiative, but that won't help you find El Dorado.'

Murphy lowered his head while wondering what else Buster might have overheard of his conversation with Caldwell. Then he smiled and reached into his pocket to finger the keys to the cells.

'I reckon you're wrong,' he said. He withdrew the keys and held them up. 'Because I'm about to show Caldwell what I can do when I use my initiative.'

CHAPTER 7

The two dead men Lincoln found in the pass had been shot. Lincoln found no signs of a prolonged gunfight, so he concluded the dead men knew their killers and this had been a dispute within the camp.

Lincoln wondered if an argument had taken place and the men he'd met beyond the trading post were fleeing from its aftermath, but he found no evidence to back up this tentative theory.

All he could work out for sure was that the men had been dead for at least a week and as with the other men their possessions hadn't been taken.

In a sombre mood he and Joshua left the pass and followed the tracks made by the prospectors in the opposite direction. As it turned out, the tracks led them away from Russell Creek, further eroding Lincoln's theory, but he remained optimistic right up until they reached hard ground and lost all sign of the tracks.

For the next day they scouted around and when

Lincoln eventually found other tracks they headed beyond the pass. The tracks were from three riders and they looked no different to the first set they'd followed.

With Lincoln in an agitated mood, and with even Joshua looking sterner than usual, they followed these tracks. They led them through another narrow pass, adding to the feeling of similarity before Lincoln confirmed that the situation was identical to the one before in the worst possible way.

They found the prospectors' camp; all three men had been shot and killed. The scene again appeared serene with the men lying beside their fire, suggesting that the attack hadn't come from an assault on the camp, but from within the camp.

Again, it didn't appear that anything had been stolen and of their attackers, they found no sign.

With no clues as to how the three separate incidents were connected, Lincoln became as quiet as Joshua. So it was with some surprise that, five days after Murphy had left to return to Russell Creek, Joshua got his attention.

'We've got company,' he said.

Lincoln rode on for several seconds before he registered what his companion had said.

Lincoln turned and sure enough, a solitary rider was approaching. The rider was too far away to discern anything about him, but as he was the first live person they'd come across since leaving the trading post, they stopped.

When the rider had moved close enough for Lincoln to confirm that Murphy had completed his mission and that the rider was Sheriff Caldwell, he noted the sheriff's angry posture.

Even Joshua leaned forward pensively as the sheriff drew up before them. Caldwell flexed a fist before opening his hand.

'For the last three days I've been all set to punch you back to Russell Creek,' Caldwell muttered. 'But as you're not on my territory no more, you get one chance to explain yourself.'

'I don't have to explain nothing to you,' Lincoln said, 'but now that you're here you can help me. We can start with what Murphy will have told you. It seems several women have gone missing from Russell Creek and they could have been taken against their will to the Scorched Land.'

'You sure do like to push your luck.' Caldwell set his hands on his hips. 'How did you learn this?'

'From Yancy Wenlock.'

'And the cost of this information?'

'Nothing, other than some expensive coffee.'

'I meant the cost to me. Yancy has fed me information for years. He does plenty wrong, but he does more good with what he tells me. Except when I met him, he told me about a US marshal making threats, so that's sure to end now.'

'I was looking for information about two prospectors we saw killed that had visited his post and that led on to the missing women. I was tempted, but I didn't threaten him, but when I find out the truth, I'll do more than just threaten.'

'I doubt any women have gone missing.' Caldwell gestured at Joshua. 'I don't blame Chastity for moving on; Salvadora fled and Mary wanted to go prospecting.'

'That's just the start. We've found two other groups of dead prospectors and—'

'I don't care about no dead gold hunters either. Those men are always shooting each other up in squabbles over gold. All I care about is my escaped prisoner, Buster McCloud.' Caldwell pointed ahead. 'He headed this way.'

Lincoln frowned. 'I'm surprised he broke out of jail.'

'He didn't. Deputy Murphy Stone released him and now the two men are on the run together.'

Lincoln shook his head. 'I'm a good judge of character and Murphy is a decent man.'

'From the little Murphy said to me, you'd fired him up with talk about taking the initiative and defying me. It seems that stretched to taking the law into his own hands.'

'I told him to follow his instincts, but I sure didn't tell him to break the law.'

Caldwell glared at Lincoln and when Lincoln met his gaze he conceded his point with a brief nod before pointing a defiant finger at him.

'I accept you wouldn't do that, but what you did was worse: you gave him ideas and they were the wrong ideas.'

'They weren't. Something bad is happening in the Scorched Land involving missing women, murdered prospectors and Domingo Villaruel. I believe they're connected and so did Murphy, even if he's trying to prove it in the wrong way.'

'And as I said, I don't believe any of that. So how can we prove who is right?'

Lincoln sighed. 'I guess by doing the one thing neither of us wants to do: we join forces and work out what's happening out here.'

With little choice, an uneasy truce descended on the two lawmen. As they rode along, they avoided looking at each other, while Joshua sported his usual sullen expression.

Despite his antipathy towards Lincoln and his theory, during his time as a lawman Caldwell had talked to many prospectors and he knew where they usually tried their luck. So he had a clearer idea about where to continue the search than Lincoln had.

Although Caldwell was looking only for the escaped Buster, Lincoln figured staying with him would help him look for the missing women, along with Domingo Villaruel.

It took them the rest of the day and the next morning before Caldwell reported that they were in the most popular area for prospecting, an area where Buster had visited before.

They had come across few signs of anyone having passed that way recently and the terrain looked no different to the other places they'd looked. Grudgingly, Lincoln accepted that without Caldwell's guidance he would probably roam around for weeks without making progress.

Caldwell led them into narrow gulches and along ravines, and they started to come across signs of habitation, although none of them was recent. In mid-afternoon they made their most promising discovery in a ravine in the form of a small camp.

Bedding was strewn around along with rotten food. Caldwell and Lincoln exchanged a few words, agreeing that the camp looked as if it had been abandoned in a hurry.

When they moved on down the ravine, they acted cautiously and spread out. Caldwell took up the lead while Lincoln took the rear and as the sun edged towards the summit of the nearest ridge, the feeling that they were getting close to discovering something proved correct.

Caldwell waved for Lincoln to hurry up, and when he joined him fifty yards from the end of the ravine, he was standing over the aftermath of another gunfight. Lincoln couldn't help but note the similarities with the previous scenes he'd discovered.

Two prospectors were lying on their backs with their chests holed. The flies had found them, but the blood on the rocks was still damp suggesting they had been killed recently, perhaps even earlier that day.

While Caldwell looked for tracks to follow, Lincoln moved around the site seeing what else he might glean from the scene.

Joshua stood over the bodies showing his usual disdain for the situation. After a short while, Lincoln noticed that he kept looking up at the high ground at the end of the ravine.

Lincoln swirled round and a moment later a gunshot rattled, the echoes ripping back and forth across the ravine. Caldwell went down on his haunches while looking around, clearly struggling to identify the shooter's location, but Lincoln decided to back Joshua's judgement and he hurried on to the exit.

For once Joshua moved quickly and he slipped in beside him. With their heads down they reached the base of the slope without further gunfire.

Lincoln hunkered down and glanced over his shoulder. Caldwell was now looking at the higher ground and when he saw that he had Lincoln's attention, he pointed at a ledge thirty yards up the slope.

Using only hand gestures Lincoln ordered Joshua to approach the ledge from beneath and to the left while he worked up to a higher position on the right.

He was unsure if Joshua would follow his command, and sure enough Joshua didn't move. Instead he peered at a boulder. When Lincoln saw what had interested him, he smiled.

There were spots of blood on the boulder and now that he'd seen the stains, he picked out others on boulders further up the slope. Figuring that he might now be facing an unknown number of wounded and desperate men, Lincoln moved on cautiously.

Further down the ravine Caldwell edged towards them and so, with people moving in, a gunman showed himself. He blasted out rapid gunshots, forcing them to dive to the ground.

When Lincoln noted that the shots had been so badly aimed that they'd all hammered into the dirt dozens of yards away from their targets, he got up and hurried up the slope.

The moment he'd stopped firing the gunman dropped back down, his quick movement giving Lincoln the impression he was the only one up there and that he was so badly wounded he was struggling to control his actions.

Lincoln still took a cautious route up the slope and when he was level with the ledge he risked peering around a boulder. What he saw confirmed that he didn't need to go any higher.

Only one gunman was on the ledge and his wild shooting had exhausted him. He was now lying on his back with his arms and legs spread-eagled and his gun lying at his side.

Lincoln aimed at him, and then gestured at Caldwell, signifying that the situation was in hand and he should hurry on to join him. When Caldwell arrived at the end of the ledge, he covered the gunman and so Lincoln hurried on to the shooter.

He kicked the gun aside and then stood over the wounded man, who registered his presence with a pained cringe. Then he tried to move away by kicking out with his legs, but he couldn't gain traction on the rock and he flopped down to lie with his eyes closed and his head rocked back.

With all the fight appearing to go out of him, Lincoln hunkered down beside him. Blood coated the man's jacket as it did most of the ledge, suggesting he'd taken up various positions and at each he'd bled some more.

'There's plenty more of us out here,' the man murmured. He'd clearly tried to use a defiant tone, but the words emerged as a pained wheeze. 'You'll not get away with this.'

'I'm not trying to get away with anything. I'm US Marshal Lincoln Hawk and I aim to work out what's going on here.'

The man opened his eyes and then blinked rapidly. He still looked past Lincoln with his eyes rolling, as if he couldn't focus.

'I'm Wilson Nesbit. I never expected to meet a lawman.'

'Even though you have, whether I save you before you spill your last drop of blood depends on your answer to this question: Who are those dead men down there?'

The implied accusation made Wilson glare at Lincoln.

'They're my colleagues. We were attacked from the top of the ridge over there. We never saw who did it.'

'You must have an idea who attacked you and why.'

'I don't know nothing.'

'In the last few days I've come across several groups of shot-up prospectors, and they didn't put up much of a fight, so I figure they knew their attackers.'

'Like I said: I don't know nothing.'

Lincoln had heard this sentiment enough times to know when the speaker was hiding something, but in this case Wilson was so weak he didn't press the matter. He signified for Caldwell to help him.

With Caldwell taking his legs and Lincoln his arms, they carried Wilson down to the bottom of the slope. They laid him in a warming patch of low sunlight that slipped through the end of the ravine.

'Wilson is a prospector,' Lincoln said when Caldwell stood back. 'But he wasn't helpful.'

Caldwell nodded and, picking up on Lincoln's ruse to make Wilson more helpful, he replied loudly.

'That's too bad,' he said. 'The more help Wilson can offer us, the better chance we have of getting him to someone who can help him.'

'I know. I fear we may have no choice but to leave him. I doubt he'll survive for long when whoever attacked his friends returns.'

Caldwell winced as Lincoln overdid the encouraging banter, but it had the desired effect when Wilson rocked his head to the side to look at them.

'Get me to El Dorado,' he said. 'Someone there will be able to help me.'

Lincoln looked at Caldwell, who shook his head.

'El Dorado isn't a real place,' Caldwell said. 'It's a myth, a place where there's enough gold to satisfy any prospector.'

'It's not,' Wilson said and pointed to the north. 'It's real.'

Caldwell snorted and loomed over Wilson. 'I believe you even less than the marshal does, so if you want to live, you'll tell us the truth, and you'll start by telling us who attacked you.'

'I never saw them.' With a grunt of effort Wilson raised himself on to an elbow and pointed a shaking finger at Caldwell. 'But know this: I thought you were them coming back to finish me off. You're not, but that just means they're still out there.'

After his long speech Wilson flopped back down on his back. Caldwell looked through the ravine exit while Lincoln looked up the side of the ridge.

'I don't see anyone,' Lincoln said. 'I reckon the killers have moved on in search of their next target.'

'Agreed,' Caldwell said. He sighed. 'So I guess if we want to get answers out of Wilson, we need to find this mythical place.'

CHAPTER 8

By the time Lincoln had decided Wilson didn't have a bullet in him and had bandaged his chest wound, the sun had set, and so they decided to stay where they were.

They found soft ground to bury the bodies and then made camp. After his burst of animation when they'd found him, Wilson reverted to silence and then dozed.

Lincoln judged that letting him rest was all they could do for him, and he wasn't optimistic they would be able to get him to help quickly. Wilson's vague direction that they would find El Dorado to the north was all he had managed to tell them, and Caldwell had no idea where to look.

Worse, the small amount of progress they'd made by finding Wilson hadn't made Caldwell any more relaxed.

'Even if you don't know where this place is,' Lincoln said when they had lit a fire, 'you'll have more ideas about where to look than I do.'

'I do,' Caldwell said, 'but that doesn't change the fact I'm not getting any closer to finding Buster.'

'I don't reckon this is a distraction. You reckon Murphy left with Buster, and Murphy was enthused about finding Domingo Villaruel, so I reckon they've both gone in search of him, and it's possible he's holed up in El Dorado.'

Caldwell shook his head. 'I don't see why Buster would want to find Domingo. It won't help him wriggle out of what's coming to him.'

'Buster had a reason for killing Aaron Knight, and it's possible Aaron is connected to Domingo—'

'Enough!' Caldwell snapped. 'You won't convince me your story is what really happened.'

Lincoln shrugged. 'Bearing in mind the alternative, I hope you're right.'

Caldwell grunted that he agreed and on that note they settled down for the night.

Lincoln had wanted to move on quickly in the morning, but as it turned out, Wilson wasn't fit enough to sit a horse. His brow was damp and he was restless. Lincoln searched through the equipment left by Wilson and his friends. He found two poles and so he stretched a blanket between them and used rope to keep the wounded man from slipping to the ground.

He doubted Wilson would be comfortable, but with this contraption attached to Wilson's horse they moved off. Joshua and Lincoln flanked Wilson, but as they could only move him at a slow pace, whenever they came across an interesting spot to search, Caldwell left them to scout around.

He explored for short distances along valleys and up ridges before returning, ensuring they could cover as much distance as possible in the hope they might have some luck.

Every hour Lincoln stopped to check on Wilson and give him water. Each time he questioned him about El Dorado, but other than vaguely pointing north, he offered no clues.

By the fifth time he'd asked without learning anything, Lincoln decided that Wilson wasn't just being vague because of his injury. He didn't know where El Dorado was.

Lincoln stopped asking and concentrated on the surroundings as he tried to work out where such a place might be. Not all the people who came here knew about El Dorado, so it had to be well hidden, but it also had to be somewhere that could be found by those who knew where to look.

He looked for obvious landmarks that could be seen from a distance. He didn't notice anything out of the ordinary and so on a hunch he drew back to let Joshua draw ahead.

Their mainly silent companion rarely offered to help or showed any apparent interest in their mission, but on several occasions he had been astute in spotting where danger might come from. So Lincoln watched Joshua, seeing if he paid particular attention to anything.

Lincoln noted that he often looked to the west, although not at any one point, suggesting he could be looking for something. When Caldwell next joined them, Lincoln drew them to a halt and while he checked on Wilson, he called the sheriff over and explained his theory.

Caldwell provided a curt nod, conveying more approval of Lincoln's actions than at any other stage in their journey together so far.

'He was always haranguing prospectors about their wickedness,' Caldwell said. 'It's possible he learned things about them.'

With Caldwell appearing more amenable, Lincoln lowered his voice and mentioned the one element of their mission he hadn't told him about so far.

'Whether you believe the missing women are here or not, Joshua appears to believe it, and if he finds Chastity, I'm not sure he means to help her.'

'I'll bear that in mind.' Caldwell turned to move away, but then turned back. 'But only if you turn out to be right.'

When they moved off, Caldwell veered westward and seized the first opportunity to move to higher ground. This route took them over rocky ground and so Lincoln ensured that Wilson's horse moved slowly.

By the time Caldwell reached the summit of the first rise, he was several hundred yards ahead of Lincoln. He stopped, looked ahead, and then turned to face the marshal, his posture eager as he leaned forward in the saddle.

As the scene beyond the rise came into sight, Lincoln saw the reason for Caldwell's behaviour. Several other rises lay ahead until the land dropped and then flattened out; set in the plains were two large pinnacles of rock.

From the direction of their approach the spires were visible as two distinct rock formations, giving the impression of a gateway. Lincoln couldn't see anything of interest beyond the rocks, but by the time he joined Caldwell he was smiling.

He waited until Caldwell acknowledged, with a brief smile, that this discovery was an interesting development, and then swung his head to the side to contemplate Joshua, who was also looking at the rocks.

'Hell's Gate?' he called out to him.

'Which is where the damned go,' Joshua said before moving on.

Caldwell nodded, a broader smile appearing, showing he didn't need an explanation that Joshua had often claimed the prospectors would head through the gates of hell.

Lincoln judged that if they didn't have to ride slowly for Wilson's sake, they could reach Hell's Gate before sundown, but as it was they only reached the last rise before the plains before they had to stop.

They made camp and Lincoln checked on Wilson's bandages. Wilson hadn't lost any blood during the day and was more responsive than before, although he still didn't reply to Lincoln's questions about El Dorado.

As the light level fell, while Joshua sat and read his Bible, Lincoln and Caldwell sat in a position where they could examine the plains. They debated where their destination might be once they'd reached the spires and although they were too far away to come up with a solution, Caldwell volunteered to ride on ahead the following day.

With that decision made, they settled down for the night. Both men were used to being alert in any circumstance and so they didn't keep watch. Instead, they rested up on either side of the fire in positions where they'd hear any intruders coming from the plains or over the land they had just traversed.

As it turned out, when Lincoln heard movement it came from close by. Joshua got up and strode towards him. Lincoln watched him approach with bemusement, but Joshua had his gaze set on the darkening plains beyond.

Bearing in mind Joshua's ability to sniff out trouble, Lincoln got up on his haunches and peered ahead. He detected nothing untoward, but that didn't stop Joshua moving past him.

When he realized that Joshua wasn't going to stop, Lincoln hurried forward and grabbed his arm, halting him.

'What's wrong?' he asked.

'If I must go through Hell's Gate, then I won't turn away,' Joshua proclaimed while looking ahead.

'You don't have to go alone. We'll reach it tomorrow.'

'Unhand me.'

Lincoln searched for anything else he could say to calm Joshua, and then with a shrug he raised his hand. The moment he released him Joshua moved off, his shoulders set forward and his gait assured.

Within a dozen paces he reached lower ground and started to disappear from view.

'Is that fool coming back?' Caldwell asked from closer to the fire.

'I don't know. He didn't say.' Lincoln turned. 'You reckon we should go after him?'

'He's unarmed, afoot, and I doubt he knows what he's doing. I reckon we'll reach Hell's Gate before him and long before he can do any harm.'

'Maybe, but he often appeared to sense things.' Lincoln shrugged when Caldwell looked doubtful. 'Or at the very least he knew things he wasn't prepared to tell us about.'

'If you want to get him back, you're doing it on your own.'

Lincoln nodded, although he couldn't shake the thought that Joshua had often acted in a manner that had appeared odd, but then later something would happen to prove he had been right.

'Get down,' he said, his voice low.

'What's wrong?'

'I don't know. Find the shadows and wait.'

Caldwell still didn't move and so Lincoln took his

own advice. He dropped down to his knees and peered around cautiously.

This action made Caldwell lower himself. Then, confirming Lincoln's fear, gunfire rattled, the sounds close together and seemingly coming from several directions.

He saw dust kick between Caldwell and the fire, the poorly aimed shots suggesting Lincoln's defensive action had hurried the shooters into acting before they were ready.

Caldwell must have had the same thought as he dashed back to the fire and kicked dirt over it before hunkering down. He peered away from the plains and so Lincoln looked in the other direction.

Then a second volley peeled out. The reports were clearly coming from his side. Lincoln turned and narrowed his eyes.

He saw movement in the gloom; at least four figures were slipping closer. He turned to get Caldwell's attention and then winced.

Caldwell was peering in the other direction. Through the gathering darkness several other figures were moving closer on that side of the camp, too.

CHAPTER 9

'Now that we're here,' Murphy said with dismay, 'I reckon I could have found this place without you.'

Buster had stopped before two pinnacles of rock that towered above them. He considered Murphy's rebuke with a smile.

'Finding these rocks is the easy part,' Buster said. 'Like I told you back in the jailhouse, you could ride within fifty yards of El Dorado and still not find it.'

Buster gestured ahead, inviting Murphy to lead the way and prove he was right, but Murphy conceded Buster's claim with a nod and held a hand out for him to lead.

Their journey from Russell Creek hadn't been as fraught as Murphy had feared it might be. His decision to release Buster had been hasty, acting on the instincts that Marshal Hawk had urged him to trust, but so far he'd not had cause to regret it.

Buster had insisted they take his prospecting equipment, and then they had headed to the Scorched

Land. He had chosen a direction with more assurance than Lincoln had shown, and Buster's resolute attitude had only reinforced Murphy's view that the former prisoner had told him the truth.

Now feeling guilty for having cast doubt on Buster's advice, Murphy slipped in behind Buster as he moved on towards the right-hand rock pillar. When Buster reached the rock's shadow, he stopped and looked to either side.

Murphy thought he was using the long shadow from the low sun to orient himself, but then he noticed that Buster was looking further afield. When Buster moved on, Murphy stopped in the same position.

He couldn't see any distinctive landmarks, although when Buster moved away from the rock at an angle, he noted that behind him was a notch in the undulating line of distant hills. He memorized the scene and then moved on after Buster, who maintained a steady course.

Murphy peered past him, eager for his first sight of their destination. He still struggled to accept this place was hard to find, but as they rode across plains that were featureless for miles ahead Buster's claim increasingly felt valid.

The sun had set when, acting on no observation that Murphy had seen, Buster drew to a halt. When Murphy joined him he noted they were on a patch of rock and ahead the ground fell away sharply, but it was only into a dusty depression.

'Will we get there before nightfall?' he asked wearily.

'We sure will.' Buster laughed, clearly relishing his reply. 'We're already there.'

'This is El Dorado?' Murphy intoned.

'The near-mythical place known only to prospectors.' Buster winked. 'So just remember, we came here looking for gold and we're down on our luck.'

Murphy waited for Buster to explain, but instead Buster moved off along the edge of the rock. Murphy slipped in beside him while looking down into the depression.

He saw nothing below, so he moved closer to the edge. He saw several objects below although with his foreshortened view he couldn't discern what they were. At this confirmation that they may have, in fact, arrived at their destination, he heard voices.

The sounds came from below, and when they reached the end of the rock and swung down into the depression, the sounds grew louder.

With a disorientating change in perspective Murphy saw that they had been riding on top of an overhang and, like overturning a rock and revealing scurrying insects, underneath was a settlement.

When they reached the base of the depression, he saw that the space beneath the overhang stretched away for dozens of yards both ahead and beneath the rock. He judged that if someone were to head towards the depression from any direction, they wouldn't see it until they were almost on top of it.

'I'll accept this place is hard to find,' Murphy said, 'but for a place that thrives on secrecy, can we just ride in?'

'We've been watched for some time. If we weren't welcome, we'd be fleeing for our lives right now.'

Buster nodded, signifying that the first person to show an interest in them was heading their way. This man was armed while behind him other people had taken a break from their business to consider them.

A corralled area was at one end of the depression and so they dismounted by the gate. With Murphy's eyes now accustomed to the gloom beneath the overhang he could see that people were resting up along the whole length.

A barrier had been erected between two poles to provide shelter from the wind and sun for a third of the length of the overhang. Behind it blankets had been raised against the rock to form crude dwelling areas. He judged that maybe twenty people were there.

Buster leaned towards him. 'Stop looking around suspiciously and let me do the talking.'

'I will, but is this the full extent of El Dorado?'

'It is.'

'Then I've noticed one thing already. No women are here.'

Buster shrugged, but before he could reply the man arrived. He identified himself as Sigmund Gaunt.

'I remember you,' he said, considering Buster, 'but not your friend.'

'We met up and decided to try our luck together,' Buster said. 'It didn't work.'

'These days that's the story everyone tells.' Sigmund gestured at the men huddled around the site. 'We used to come here to boast and to trade. Now we just want protection.'

Buster provided a knowing nod, although he shot a glance at Murphy that warned him to be quiet. Murphy reckoned that Buster didn't know what Sigmund had meant, but now that he'd mentioned it, the few details he'd gathered about this place didn't match the reality.

He had expected the lawless El Dorado to be filled with trigger-happy prospectors. He'd thought he'd have to keep his wits about him to survive for long enough to get answers about Domingo and the missing women, but nobody here looked threatening.

Everyone just looked as if they wanted somewhere warm and safe to sleep for the night.

'This might be my last visit here,' Buster said as Sigmund led them under the overhang.

'Then I hope you can get away, but it might be best to wait until Domingo returns. He might have had better luck this time.'

'What's he doing?' Buster offered a smile when Sigmund stopped abruptly and directed a bemused look at them. 'We've hardly seen anyone since the last time I was here, so I don't know what Domingo is concerning himself with now.'

'The war!' Sigmund said before reducing the

impact of his declaration with a shrug. 'Or whatever we should call a battle against raiders who are trying to kill every prospector.'

'Who's doing it?'

Sigmund looked from one man to the other while narrowing his eyes.

'Are you really claiming you don't know we're in the middle of a fight for our lives?'

Buster frowned, clearly struggling to find an answer that wouldn't deepen Sigmund's suspicion, and so Murphy spoke up.

'Last week I came across two prospectors who were fleeing for their lives,' he said. 'They got shot up, so I hightailed it out of there before the killers saw me. I met Buster and we joined forces, but we thought that incident was only a score being settled.'

'Scores are being settled, and we're hearing of more every day. Where was this attack?'

Murphy described the incident he'd seen while he'd been with Marshal Hawk, and with him providing some truthful elements after Buster's guarded answers, Sigmund relaxed.

When Murphy had finished, Sigmund directed them to a corner of the overhang and then left to deal with their horses.

They sat with their backs to the rock, and with nobody coming within a dozen yards of them Buster explained how El Dorado operated. The travellers who just wanted a place to stay for a few days congregated at one end and nearest the edge, while the permanent residents stayed further under the over-hang behind the barrier.

With Domingo and his men being elsewhere, the former group outnumbered the latter. Although the place had gained a reputation for trading, the people didn't mingle and everyone sat either on their own or in small groups.

Once Murphy had settled down and taken in the situation, he confirmed his earlier observation, making him shuffle towards Buster.

'I was right,' he said. 'I can't see any women here.'

'I know,' Buster said. 'Then again, I never saw any when I was last here.'

'So do you reckon Domingo hasn't brought the women here?'

'It's too early to say that. When I was last here I wasn't on the lookout for any women.' Buster pointed to the opposite end of the overhang. 'But beyond that barrier are several caves. Domingo and others went there at night. I heard it was for gambling and I stayed away, but that might not explain everything that goes on there.'

Murphy nodded and then lowered his head to ground level so that he could see more of the sky.

'It's getting dark, so we should explore now while we can still see what's in those caves.'

'We're sure to be seen and we'll look suspicious.'

'We will, but rooting around in the dark will look even more suspicious and besides, we won't learn anything by being cautious.'

Buster rubbed his jaw and then gave a brief nod. He moved to rise while peering at the route they would have to take, but then sat down again quickly.

'I reckon we should wait after all,' he said.

When Murphy saw what had concerned him, he joined him in adopting their previous positions of sitting with their backs against the rock.

Several riders were coming down into the depression. Domingo Villaruel was leading the group. The moment Domingo dismounted several men from the far extent of the overhang hurried over.

While their horses were led away to the corral at one end of the depression, a brief conversation ensued that made others gravitate towards them.

Murphy couldn't hear what was said, but everyone's downbeat posture told him what had happened. They had failed to find the raiders and that would only increase tensions.

Sigmund Gaunt got Domingo's attention and gestured at them. Murphy presumed he was letting him know who had arrived while he'd been gone, but the conversation carried on for some time.

'Trouble,' Murphy whispered.

'Don't panic yet,' Buster said. 'Keep your head down and let me do the talking.'

Buster edged forward so that he could intercept Domingo, but as it turned out, Domingo accepted what he'd been told and moved diagonally across the space beneath the overhang. When he'd passed by them, Murphy sighed with relief.

'Sigmund probably just told him I'd come across other shot-up prospectors.'

'He'll have heard that story a lot recently.' Buster stood up. 'But with everyone moving around, I reckon we should investigate now.'

Murphy nodded. Exploring at any time could lead to problems, but Domingo's return had encouraged everyone to be more animated and so they were less likely to be noticed.

Acting in a nonchalant manner they moved through the group that had gathered around Domingo. When these people didn't pay them any attention, they slipped out of the overhang and into the depression.

Several men from Domingo's group were making their way out of the depression, presumably to stand guard in case the raiders arrived. Feigning concern, Murphy and Buster walked along while looking up to ground level.

When they'd moved in front of the barrier, Murphy saw three caves. They all had small entrances and in the fading light they didn't look promising.

They wandered to the other side of the depression in an apparently casual stroll while Murphy kept one eye on the scene beneath the overhang. Everyone's attention was on the process of lighting torches and nobody looked their way.

Once they'd moved past the point where they could be seen from under the overhang, the guards were no longer in sight. So with a smile Buster let Murphy know that he reckoned they hadn't been noticed.

They hurried on. When they looked in the first cave, they found it stretched back for only a few yards so that even in the gloom they could see its extent and the fact that it was empty.

They moved on to the second cave, which was larger, as in the gloom they couldn't see the walls. They slipped inside and waited until their eyes accustomed to the light level. Then they separated and took one side of the cave apiece.

They moved on with each man walking with a hand out to the wall. Murphy's side was curved and after a dozen paces he approached Buster.

Again, they concluded that nobody was inside, although they found bedding that had been strewn around. They rummaged through it, but found nothing to confirm the women had slept there.

Without much hope they moved on to the final cave. This one was in the corner of the depression and had the largest opening.

The entrance pointed westward letting it take advantage of the limited light and so when they slipped inside Murphy could see most of the interior. The cave stretched back for as far as the rest of El Dorado did, but nobody was within.

More bedding along with three crates were in the centre of the cave. Murphy removed the lid from the largest crate and peered inside.

The crate was empty and a quick kick of the others confirmed they were empty, too. There was nowhere left to search within the depression and outside Murphy had seen no likely places for them to look, so he turned to Buster and received a shake of the head.

For another minute they stood silently and deep in thought until an increase in the light level alerted Murphy to a problem. He turned to the entrance as several men stepped into view.

Sigmund Gaunt held a torch aloft dazzling Murphy and ensuring he couldn't discern who else had arrived. They had agreed that if they were discovered Buster would speak up, so Buster moved forward, but he stopped when Sigmund lowered his arm and let them see that Domingo Villaruel led the group.

'What are you doing here?' Domingo demanded.

'I was showing my friend around,' Buster said. 'We're worried. We saw some trouble and we sure don't want to see any more.'

'Everyone here is worried, but you should know this is the last place you'd find anything interesting. They've all gone now.'

'You're talking about the women?'

'Of course.'

Buster gulped. 'I was looking for one in particular. Her name was Letisha.'

'Who ever cared what their names were?'

'I did. There was another one called Mary.'

Domingo furrowed his brow and then looked at Sigmund, who shrugged. Then he walked across the cave with Sigmund following him. When the light revealed Buster's face Domingo nodded.

'I remember you. When you were last here you kept yourself to yourself.' He moved on to consider Murphy. 'I've not seen you here before, but I do know the face.'

He looked him over with a quizzical expression before turning back to Sigmund. Domingo received a narrowed-eyed look, as if the conversation had concerned him.

Murphy wasn't sure what the problem was, but that issue fled from his thoughts when Domingo swirled back to face him, his wide eyes showing he'd now worked out who he was.

'Howdy, Domingo,' Murphy said.

'Deputy Murphy Stone,' Domingo said. 'I've had no luck recently, but your arrival has sure cheered me.'

Murphy bunched his fists. He tried to avoid reacting, but talking with this man made his blood race.

He ran forward and hurled himself at Domingo. He got to within two paces of him, but then Sigmund dropped his torch and hammered a round-armed blow into his stomach.

With Murphy moving forward the blow knocked all the wind out of him and he dropped to his knees before Domingo, who stepped forward to slap his cheek.

'Leave him alone,' Buster said behind him, but rapid footfalls sounded followed by a thud as Buster was knocked down.

Domingo glanced at the altercation and then turned back to Murphy, who struggled to speak as he gasped for air. Domingo laughed and swung back his fist.

'And now I can make someone else suffer,' he said.

CHAPTER 10

Lincoln fast-crawled to the best cover he could find – a rounded boulder. It was only two feet high, but a depression to one side let him hug the ground with some feeling of security.

By the gutted fire, Caldwell followed Lincoln's lead in seeking cover behind a boulder. This one was large enough to let him hunker down and peer over the top at the people who were moving in on his side.

With the last flames from the fire spluttering out, the darkness deepened and so Lincoln could only make out the outlines of the numerous forms that were scurrying into cover.

They had made camp on a high point and so when the shooters went to ground further down the slope, they disappeared from view. Lincoln saw enough of them while they were taking up positions to note that they were lying down on both sides of their camp and beyond the fire.

This suggested they were leaving the route down to the plains open, but as that might be a trap Lincoln resolved to follow Joshua in that direction only as a last resort.

Lincoln caught Caldwell's attention with a wave and then using hand gestures they agreed where most of the newcomers were. They had both seen several people that the other hadn't noticed meaning at least a dozen raiders were out there.

Worse, neither man was sure of anyone's exact location.

Long moments passed quietly. Lincoln reckoned that with the element of surprise lost, the people were either waiting for them to make a mistake by moving or waiting for the cover of darkness.

The latter was approaching fast and so Lincoln looked for the next nearest cover. He figured that if he could reach a different position unseen, when the assault came he could spring a surprise on them.

Accordingly, he noted that they'd left Wilson beside a mound that protected him from the prevailing wind that whipped up from the plains. Lincoln lowered his head and with his body pressed to the ground, he snaked out of the depression.

At first he moved slowly so that if he was spotted he could hurry back to his former position, but he covered two body lengths without reprisals. As he reckoned it was already dark enough to mask his movements, he speeded up.

Caldwell ignored his action and he even glanced at

Lincoln's former position several times to support the subterfuge.

Lincoln kept his head down and only looked up to check on his progress. With every passing moment the darkness deepened and so he could no longer see Wilson's form and could only discern the mound as being a lighter patch of earth five body lengths ahead.

He had become used to the quiet and so when a gun report sounded, he couldn't help but flinch. Moving only his eyes he glanced around, but he saw no movement.

Caldwell raised himself and fired over his covering boulder before dropping down.

A moment later a rapid volley of shots ripped into the boulder forcing him to stay down while other shots whistled into the earth a few yards ahead of Lincoln.

Lincoln grunted in irritation as it looked as if his movements had been tracked and so he abandoned his stealthy approach. He got up on haunches and with his head down, he sprinted for the mound.

He covered half the distance before gunfire tore out making him thrust his head down even further. The action unbalanced him and he fell forward, forcing him to put out a hand to stop himself from falling over before stumbling on.

With scrambling, frantic paces he ran into the mound shoulder first where he steadied himself. Two quick shots rang out, but Lincoln couldn't tell what their target had been and so he looked at Wilson.

A sudden wind made the fire splutter into life and he winced on seeing blood glisten. Wilson's chest had been holed repeatedly, suggesting the previous gunfire had all been aimed at him.

Figuring that meant his current position wasn't as secure as he'd hoped, Lincoln scrambled around the side of the mound. Two gunshots hurried him on his way and ensured he kept his head down when he reached the other side.

Here, even the weak firelight didn't reach and so he cautiously snaked his body higher and peered over the top.

Caldwell was kneeling down with his body hunched up close to his covering boulder and his cautious glances to either side showed he had yet to pick out a target.

Lincoln joined him in looking around, but he failed to see anyone. Several minutes passed without incident making Lincoln unsure what the attackers' plan was.

Bearing in mind these were probably the people who had killed the other prospectors and had just killed Wilson, Lincoln decided to test the theory that this might be a private feud and that he and Caldwell weren't their targets.

'What do you people want?' he called.

Long moments passed and then someone spoke up from the darkness.

'That depends on who you are.'

The response had come from a boulder ten yards

beyond Caldwell, and something about the tone of voice surprised Lincoln.

'I'm US Marshal Lincoln Hawk and the other man is Sheriff Caldwell from Russell Creek.'

'In that case if you want to live, throw down your guns and surrender.'

The second statement had again been delivered in a harsh manner, but the tone was lighter than he'd expected and so he glanced at Caldwell, who was looking at him with a furrowed brow.

'The speaker sounded young,' Caldwell said, his voice low and just carrying to Lincoln.

'I don't reckon so,' Lincoln said. 'It sounded like a woman to me.'

'You're wrong,' Caldwell mouthed, although his frown acknowledged that he had doubts.

'We're lawmen,' Lincoln shouted. 'We don't take orders from killers.'

A rapid volley of shots hammered out, coming from all directions and giving Lincoln no choice but to keep his head down behind the mound.

After the first few gunshots he noted that the firing was aimed around his position with no shot hitting the ground within three feet of him, and so he looked up.

'We can see you clearly and every one of those bullets could have hit you,' the voice from the hidden leader bellowed. 'Throw down your guns or the next volley will do just that.'

This time Lincoln was sure that the speaker was a

woman. He glanced around, and although he didn't doubt that the attackers had a clear view of him, he couldn't see them. With a sigh, he stood up and stepped out from behind the mound.

He held his hands wide apart as he caught Caldwell's eye. With a resigned nod Caldwell followed Lincoln's lead.

They both dropped their guns, but neither man moved away from their weapons as they waited for the attackers' next move.

Muttering sounded in the darkness and then footfalls pattered as someone hurried closer.

The fire hadn't died out completely and by the light of the few flames, Lincoln watched a woman approach. She scurried towards Caldwell, and when he saw her Caldwell twitched with surprise.

She moved on to the fire and went to her knees to coax the flames back to life. As the light level improved, Lincoln saw the rest of the attackers edging closer; they, too, were women.

They were all armed and aiming guns at the two lawmen. When they formed an arc before them, the leader moved round to stand before Caldwell.

'What are you doing here?' Caldwell asked.

'I could ask you the same question,' the woman said with a small smile playing on her lips.

Caldwell shook his head and with him not saying any more, Lincoln spoke up.

'You know this woman?' he said.

Caldwell turned to him and raised an eyebrow, his

delay in replying letting Lincoln accept that the explanation he was trying hard not to consider was in fact the truth.

'You came here to look for Salvadora Somoza,' Caldwell said nodding at the leader, 'but it seems she found you. And over there is Chastity, Joshua's daughter.'

Lincoln looked along the line to a young woman who raised a hand briefly.

'And Mary?' Lincoln asked, his query making another woman nod.

Caldwell snorted a rueful laugh. 'So it seems I was right after all. The women didn't need rescuing.'

'Except they did,' Salvadora said, 'and I was the woman to do it.'

'Are you saying Domingo Villaruel kidnapped them and so you took him on?'

Salvadora nodded. 'I reckoned something was amiss when women from the Lucky Horseshoe saloon kept disappearing, but I wasn't sure of the details until Aaron Knight told me what was in store for me. Before he could act, Buster McCloud came looking for Letisha and he shot up Aaron.'

Salvadora looked at the line of women, and another one nodded, confirming her identity.

'So you came here?' Lincoln asked.

'Aaron told me Domingo took the women to El Dorado and so I staked out the place. I remembered who the feisty ones were, who might have the courage to fight back and, one memorable night, we did just that.'

'We chose our moment when Domingo wasn't there,' Letisha said, stepping forward. 'Now we're taking down his empire one man at a time.'

'So you killed the dead prospectors we've come across?'

'Sure. We remembered the ones who deserved to die and we made them regret what they did to us.' Letisha sneered before softening her expression. 'But we're not as cruel as the ones who paid for us even though they knew we were being held in El Dorado against our will. We've done no harm to those who did us no harm.'

Salvadora swirled round to glare at Letisha, seemingly preparing to disagree with her. Although she said nothing, her narrowed eyes suggested that Letisha had referred to an old argument and that perhaps this group wasn't as united as they had first appeared.

'So Wilson had to die?' Lincoln asked.

'He paid for his crime.'

'And us?'

Letisha looked at Salvadora, and so their leader spoke up.

'It sounds as if you came here to help us,' she said. 'We're grateful for that. Once we've completed our mission, you can leave.'

'And that mission is to kill Domingo Villaruel?'

'We fled El Dorado, but for the last week we've been working our way back. We're now confident we can destroy that place and anyone who stands with Domingo.'

'From what I've heard about Domingo, that's a noble aim.' Lincoln waited until Salvadora nodded and then took a pace to the side to stand over his gun. 'But dealing with men like him is the duty of the law, not the people who reckon they've been wronged.'

Making his movements slowly Lincoln lowered his hand towards his gun. Nobody reacted and so he bent down while still moving his hand.

He was starting to think they'd let him take the weapon when Salvadora snapped up her gun arm. She tore out a shot that sliced into the ground a foot from Lincoln's questing fingers.

Lincoln's hand was six inches away from the gun and he'd back himself to reach it before she fired again, but most of the other women firmed their gun arms and so he raised his hand.

'If the law had stepped in earlier,' Salvadora said, 'this situation would never have developed.'

She cast Caldwell an accusing glare making the sheriff lower his head and then take a long step away from his own gun. With him effectively surrendering, Lincoln straightened up and moved backwards.

Lincoln spread his hands. 'We're here now to end this situation.'

'By the time we've finished with Domingo, you won't need to.' Salvadora considered him coldly and then pointed at the mound where Wilson's body lay. 'Go over there and keep quiet. If you try anything, lawmen or no lawmen, you'll get what that man got.'

Lincoln opened his mouth to continue the argument,

but Caldwell started slouching towards him and so he did as he'd been told and moved over to the mound.

Caldwell sat beside him and with their acquiescence, Salvadora organized her group. She directed two women to move Wilson aside and then ordered two more to watch over them.

Their guards stayed some distance away and so Lincoln leaned towards Caldwell.

'What's your suggestion?' he whispered.

Caldwell didn't reply immediately, appearing lost in thought.

'About what?' he said, his tone distracted.

'About taking control before more blood is shed either by the prospectors or by these women?'

'I don't reckon we can.' Caldwell sighed. 'Or should.'

'You're not saying we should let Salvadora raid El Dorado, are you?'

'I'm saying she was right. I'm responsible for this situation. If I'd have stepped in earlier, these women wouldn't have suffered.'

'You're not to blame for something that happened this far away from Russell Creek.'

'And yet I am. I should have pieced this together. You worked it out, it seems Buster McCloud figured out what was happening and even my idiot deputy knew something was wrong.'

Lincoln glanced around the camp as he wondered what he could say to make Caldwell stop feeling sorry for himself. But their conversation had made their guards edge forward, and so he limited himself to patting Caldwell on the back.

'Buster and your deputy made mistakes, but in the end, they did what they thought was the right thing.'

Caldwell considered this, and then nodded.

'As must I,' he said.

CHAPTER 11

The morning brought no change to Caldwell's depressed outlook.

After their brief talk the previous night Lincoln had failed to get him to speak again. So he'd got a full night's sleep, ensuring that he was rested while hopefully making his captors off-guard.

The morning didn't bring any change to the women's plan and Salvadora set about organizing them to leave and head across the plains.

Lincoln had no clear plan as to how he could seize control of the situation, especially as he couldn't rely on Caldwell's help. So he kept quiet until Salvadora turned her attention to them.

'Are you going to give me any trouble?' she asked.

'Only if you don't release me,' Lincoln said.

'I feared that's the way you'd want to deal with this.'

She gestured and the women must have agreed their actions beforehand as two women moved in carrying rope. Lincoln accepted this development without complaint or struggle, but he sat up straight.

With him appearing alert, the women moved cautiously, which was the effect he wanted to achieve as he hoped they wouldn't tie his bonds tightly. Then they moved on to Caldwell, and when the sheriff stayed still Lincoln reckoned he received an extra twist of the ropes before they were drawn tight and tied.

Only when the women stood back did Salvadora approach him. She looked over their bonds with approval and then shooed the women away to their horses.

'So you're going through with this?' Lincoln said.

'My quarrel isn't with you, so I don't want no argument. We'll either return or we won't. If we return, we'll have taken care of Domingo and so we'll free you. If we don't, we'll have failed, but I'm sure you're resourceful enough to free yourself.'

'There's a limit to what we can do, and when you get yourself killed, the first thing Domingo will do is scout around to see if any more of you are left, and then he'll find us.'

Salvadora narrowed her eyes, clearly wondering what trap Lincoln was trying to lay before dismissing the matter and moving towards the horses. Letisha had yet to mount up and must have been listening to their conversation as she drew Salvadora aside.

The two women talked with occasional glances at them and at the mounted women. The result of their debate came when Salvadora nodded and Letisha smiled, suggesting she had talked Salvadora round to her way of thinking.

Then Salvadora beckoned two women, Mary and Chastity, to get down off their horses, which they did in short order and with relieved expressions. Salvadora ushered them away to stand before the lawmen.

'I'll leave these two with you,' she said. 'If we don't return, they'll free you.'

Lincoln acknowledged her action with a nod, but then fixed her with his firm gaze.

'You've suffered, but if you go through with this, I'll have to come after you and I don't want to do that.'

'If you do, you'll get what Domingo will get.'

Salvadora returned his resolute gaze and then turned on her heel. She joined Letisha in mounting up and then swiftly led the women off.

Lincoln watched the group until they disappeared beyond the edge of the slope down to the plains and then considered the women who had stayed with them. They both relaxed their postures at the same time reinforcing his earlier observation that they were relieved to have been left behind.

For a while he said nothing, ensuring he didn't squander his chances of talking them round before he'd picked up more clues as to why Salvadora's plans hadn't enthused them as much as they had motivated the others.

The two women settled down ten yards away where they could watch them while chatting to each other. Their tones were nervous with frequent glances their way, and neither woman held a weapon.

Lincoln tried to catch Caldwell's eye, but the sheriff ignored him and so he cleared his throat. When this was ignored he coughed again and so Mary got the idea and brought him a ladle of water, which he gulped down.

'Thank you,' he said and then settled down while smiling.

Five minutes passed before his calm demeanour had the desired effect.

'If this goes wrong, we will let you go,' Mary said.

'I know. Murphy spoke well of you.'

She glanced at Caldwell before nodding.

'I liked him. He was a good man.'

'He still is. He was worried about what happened to you.'

'He shouldn't have been.' She looked over her shoulder towards the plains. 'We didn't suffer like most of the other women did.'

'Why was that?'

'Domingo Villaruel didn't kidnap either of us. I joined some prospectors.' She turned to Chastity, presumably so she could provide her story, but she didn't speak up. 'It was the same for Chastity.'

'So why are you with Salvadora?'

'She and her group arrived. The men weren't concerned and they invited them to join the camp. Then she killed them.' She sighed. 'That's what happened to Chastity's group, too.'

'It was,' Chastity said, this time taking the opportunity

to explain. 'The men I was with were no saints, but they didn't deserve what happened to them.'

Lincoln nodded. 'Those women suffered and they were right to fight back, but Salvadora has taken this too far.'

'You can't blame her. She suffered at Domingo's hands.'

The two women looked at each, this clearly being a subject they'd debated before.

'I'm not denying that, but her plans can do more harm than good,' Lincoln said.

He prompted by glancing at his bound hands, but that appeared to have been a bad move as both women shook their heads.

'We're not defying her,' Mary said.

Lincoln reckoned that her statement had more to do with fear than loyalty, but he reckoned he'd done enough for now. He reverted to silence, but Caldwell showed an interest in proceedings for the first time in a while.

'Then that's bad news for your friend Murphy,' he said. 'He's headed to El Dorado.'

Mary winced. 'He's made a bad mistake, but he's never been there before, so he has nothing to fear from Salvadora.'

'It sounds as if the prospectors you joined should have had nothing to fear from her, but she still killed them.'

'I know why she did it; she won't harm a good man like Murphy.'

Caldwell appeared to accept her viewpoint with a shrug and then looked at Chastity.

'And what about a good man like your father?'

'What's he got. . . ?' Chastity trailed off and closed her eyes for a moment. 'He followed me.'

'He was with us until just before Salvadora arrived. By my reckoning, he should arrive at Hell's Gate at about the same time that Salvadora does. I hope she's minded to listen to him.'

Chastity gulped and lowered her head. Then, without looking at Mary, she moved over to stand before Caldwell.

'Can you make sure he's safe?' She gestured at Mary. 'And Murphy, too?'

'I was wrong to only run Domingo Villaruel out of town and I was wrong not to work out what Aaron Knight was doing to help him. I'll make sure no more innocents suffer.'

Chastity nodded and then set to work loosening his bonds. Mary watched her and then with a resigned sigh moved over to Lincoln and started work on the rope that bound his wrists.

Nobody spoke while the women freed the lawmen. Then, without discussion, they headed to their horses.

The lawmen moved slowly as they stomped feeling back into their limbs and so the women mounted up first. When they rode off, Lincoln nodded to Caldwell.

'You did well,' he said. 'I was failing to talk them round.'

'I just told them the truth.'

Lincoln nodded as he mounted his horse.

'And that's not a palatable truth. We'll find it hard to stop Salvadora while still bringing Domingo to justice.'

Caldwell frowned as he mounted up, and then turned to him.

'I don't intend to stop Salvadora. I intend to help her wipe out Domingo and Buster and my double-crossing deputy and all the other no-good varmints out there.'

Caldwell waited while Lincoln considered him with surprise and then hurried his horse on after the women. Lincoln drew in behind him, figuring that if they were to resolve the situation they couldn't afford to waste time arguing.

Once they reached the lower ground, Mary and Chastity headed for Hell's Gate. As Salvadora had led the women off more than an hour ago, Lincoln didn't look out for them and with everyone eager to reach their destination they made good time.

The sun was at its highest when they approached the two sentinel rocks. For the first time the women consulted each other before looking around and then choosing a direction.

When they'd swung round the rocks and were riding away, Lincoln hurried on to join them.

'How long will it take to get there?' he said.

'We've never been to El Dorado,' Mary said, 'but I gather it's less than an hour from here.'

'Then we should have enough time to work something

out with Salvadora before she makes a bad mistake and gets all the women killed.'

'Why are you sure we'll get there in time?'

Lincoln pointed ahead to the open terrain.

'Because these plains afford little cover. Raiding El Dorado will take time and patience while waiting for the right moment.'

'I don't know what her full plan is, but I don't reckon she was planning to wait before taking on Domingo.'

'You mean she'll just ride up to El Dorado in full daylight and start shooting away?'

Mary frowned and looked at Chastity, who shrugged.

'That plan has worked well so far,' Chastity said. 'Although before she had the advantage that the men she attacked weren't expecting trouble.'

Lincoln winced. 'In other words, she's become overconfident.'

He didn't wait for an answer and with the direction the women were taking now becoming clear, he hurried his horse on. Behind him, Caldwell spoke briefly to the women before galloping on to join him.

'She may be wrong, but don't try to stop her,' he said.

Lincoln shook his head. 'If we don't get there before she starts her raid that's one argument we won't need to have.'

CHAPTER 12

'Get out here,' Domingo Villaruel demanded.

He received only silence from within the cave and so muttered low orders to Sigmund, who grunted that he agreed.

Standing on either side of the entrance, Murphy and Buster nodded to each other and prepared to use whatever opportunity came their way.

The previous night, despite his threats, Domingo had only roughed them up, after which they'd been disarmed and left in the cave.

The delay had ensured they'd spent a restless night awaiting whatever fate Domingo had in store for them, but by morning they had decided they wouldn't accept that fate without a fight. They'd broken up one of the crates to arm themselves with short lengths of wood, and then they'd waited to jump the first person to come into the cave.

They would then need to seize this person's weapon and take the situation from there. Unfortunately,

Domingo was aware they might fight back and had several men with him as he approached.

Then shuffling and thuds sounded. Inside the cave, the two men glanced at each other and shrugged, but Domingo was the first to make his intentions clear.

'Sigmund is piling up wood outside the cave,' he said. 'Come out quietly or he'll set fire to the wood and smoke you out.'

'If Domingo wants us to come out,' Murphy whispered to Buster, 'I reckon we should oblige.'

They mouthed a countdown from five and then while Sigmund was still stacking the wood, they charged through the entrance. Buster went around the right-hand side of the growing wood pile and swung his plank at Sigmund.

The intended blow didn't even hit its target as two men moved in on him from behind and bundled him to the ground. Murphy had more luck as fewer men were standing on his side of the pile.

He clattered the plank against one man's side and jabbed the end into another's man stomach, but then Sigmund moved in. He grabbed Murphy's arm with one hand and dashed the plank from his hand with the other. Then he shoved him into the pile of wood.

Murphy floundered amongst the twigs and branches before shoving wood aside to fight his way clear. By the time he'd gained his feet, Buster was being held firmly from behind while Domingo was standing before him with a gun aimed at his chest.

'I'm pleased you still have some fight in you,' he

114

said. 'It'll help you through a long day.'

Sigmund then seized Murphy and while holding his arms behind his back he marched him across the depression. They used a steep path back up to ground level that avoided moving past the overhang and when they reached the plains, Murphy got an inkling of what was in store for them.

Two stakes had been set into the ground in the nearest patch of soft ground while rope lay on the ground beside them. Two men hurried on and the moment they reached the stakes they set to work securing them.

Murphy struggled, but he couldn't dislodge Sigmund and within moments any chance of gaining freedom had gone when rope was wrapped around his chest securing him to the stake. The men had clearly worked out what they should do beforehand as they worked with efficient speed and then stood back.

Murphy looked down and confirmed that his legs, ankles and arms were wrapped in multiple coils while his hands were behind his back. Domingo waved the captors away and, with a glance around the plains, Sigmund led the men back to the depression leaving Domingo standing alone before them.

'What now?' Buster said after Domingo had considered them for a while.

Domingo licked his lips and then stood before Buster, who tensed, and then moved on to Murphy, who gulped making Domingo laugh.

'The rope should secure you, but you're ingenious

men,' Domingo said. 'So here's the deal. If you can get free before the raiders arrive, run and never come back. If you don't, you'll be the first ones the raiders kill.'

Domingo tipped his hat with a mocking salute and then turned to head back to the depression.

'That's no deal,' Buster said when Domingo's footfalls had receded into the distance. 'We'll never get free.'

Murphy wriggled, but his arms were held securely.

'And when we fail to escape,' he said unhappily, 'our deaths will provide an early warning that the raiders are coming.'

Buster grunted that he agreed with Murphy's gloomy outlook, but that didn't stop Murphy straining against the ropes. When he failed to loosen them, he tried rocking from side to side and shaking the stake, but it was driven firmly into the ground and it didn't move.

So he concentrated on trying to wriggle so that he could free an arm. The process was frustrating as every time he drew his arm to one side for a few inches, it tightened the ropes around his other arm, making him wince in pain.

From time to time he tried to judge how far he could move his arm so that he could work out if his efforts were letting him move more freely. But as he could manage only a few inches of movement, he couldn't tell if he was making progress.

'You'll never get an arm free,' Buster said after an

hour of silent straining.

'Perhaps I won't, but I'm still going to try,' Murphy said before grunting in frustration.

He stopped struggling and took deep breaths to calm himself down after his futile efforts. With his head lowered he fought to keep despair at bay.

No longer expending energy, he relaxed and paid attention to his surroundings, and from the corner of his eye he detected movement. He stilled and after a few moments he confirmed that someone was moving nearby.

Buster followed his gaze to look at a mound around twenty yards away where a hunched over form crawled out and then snaked along the ground towards them.

'It must be one of the raiders,' Buster whispered.

'In which case our only hope is to stay silent and hope they leave us alone.'

Buster nodded and then both men looked away from the newcomer. They affected bored demeanours to show that nothing was amiss with Buster lowering his head and Murphy rocking from side to side.

Presently, Murphy heard shuffling as the newcomer approached and then scraping noises coming from beside Buster's stake.

Casually, he glanced to the side and then couldn't help but flinch in surprise when he saw a woman tugging on the ropes that bound Buster's ankles. Buster noticed his reaction, but with his flared eyes alone he conveyed that Murphy needed to act calmly.

Murphy returned a bemused look and then pointedly looked away from Buster to the depression while flexing his arms. The scraping noises continued suggesting the woman was making progress while Murphy saw no movement around El Dorado giving him hope that she hadn't been noticed.

'I'll free my arms,' Buster said after a while. 'You help out Murphy.'

The woman grunted in affirmation and then shuffling sounded as she moved on to Murphy, but Buster must have caught on for the first time that he was being freed by a woman as he gasped.

'Don't react,' Murphy said. 'I don't reckon anyone's seen what's happening out here yet.'

'What are you doing here, Letisha?' Buster whispered.

'I'll answer all your questions,' the woman, Letisha, said, her voice coming from behind Murphy's stake. 'But I really think you should listen to your friend.'

Buster muttered something under his breath, but then silenced until Murphy felt the rope around his ankles being tugged.

'You can still answer one question,' Buster said. 'Are you helping the raiders?'

'Sure. Why else do you think I've been crawling across the ground to free you?'

'But I headed here to find out what happened to you.'

'I've heard that before quite recently.'

Letisha gave a sharp tug and Murphy felt the rope

around an ankle loosen. With Buster not replying, Murphy glanced down.

'Are you the woman who went missing from Aaron Knight's house recently?' he asked.

'I am,' she said.

'Have you come across Mary?' He sighed when Letisha grunted. 'And Chastity?'

'All the women who were brought here are safe.'

'Even Salvadora?'

'Salvadora is our leader, and any minute now she'll launch an attack on El Dorado. If you want to avoid getting cut down in the crossfire, I need to free you.'

'Then carry on,' Murphy said. From the corner of his eye he noticed more movement. 'And hurry.'

CHAPTER 13

Gunfire was blasting out in the distance, but Lincoln still slowed his horse.

Salvadora had ridden towards a destination that Lincoln had still been unable to spot. She had headed towards the sun and even if she'd found cover, this direction would still have increased the chances of Domingo seeing her and the approaching women.

Accordingly, Lincoln and Caldwell looked for cover. A small depression in the ground lay ahead and so they moved down into it, finding that at the bottom it was deep enough that, once they'd dismounted, they could no longer see the plains.

They hurried on to the lip of the depression where they hunkered down to survey the scene ahead. While they'd been taking cover Lincoln had heard no more shooting and he could see no movement ahead.

They waited patiently. Ten minutes passed and then a quarter-mile ahead four men moved towards a rise. They were too far away for Lincoln to discern their intent, but they were acting stealthily while moving to a higher position.

When they settled down Lincoln could no longer see them, but his last sighting suggested they were planning to attack the bottom of the rise where, presumably, the women had holed up. With the situation looking as if it would develop soon, Lincoln glanced at Caldwell.

They had not had a chance to discuss their differences, and Caldwell's terse nod acknowledged they needed to act quickly and that this wasn't the right time to argue. So, while keeping their heads down they moved out of the depression.

By now Mary and Chastity were approaching. Lincoln waved at them to get down into the depression and to stay there.

He didn't stay to check they complied with his order and with Caldwell at his side they moved on. Their progress was slow as they sought the available cover in the gently undulating land, but Lincoln judged that they were careful enough not to attract attention.

They had halved the distance to the rise when Lincoln caught his first sight of Salvadora's group. They were hugging the dirt and looking away from the men towards a large hole in the ground.

The women had fanned out taking up positions that suggested their targets were holed up there.

'El Dorado,' Caldwell said after considering the scene.

Lincoln narrowed his eyes as he looked around before ending his perusal peering at the hole.

'You reckon that hole in the ground is this mythical place?'

Caldwell stopped and sought cover by kneeling down. When Lincoln joined him in keeping down, Caldwell nodded.

'It's been said you could ride within fifty yards of El Dorado and not see it. Maybe a hole in the ground of the kind we stopped in would explain that.'

'Which means Salvadora would be in a good position to pin everyone down, if it wasn't for the men lurking behind her.'

Caldwell nodded. 'When the men on the rise act, she'll be trapped.'

'So this is the moment when you need to decide who you'll help.'

'I've already done that. I'll finally take care of Domingo. Then I'll move on to dealing with Buster and my double-crossing deputy.'

'You do that, but just remember that our primary aim here is to keep the peace.'

Caldwell narrowed his eyes, now seemingly ready to have an overdue argument about who was in charge and who was in the right, but before he could retort the first gunshot in a while sounded ahead. Lincoln winced and raised his head as more retorts ripped out.

He expected to see that the men on the rise had finally made their move, but for a moment he couldn't tell what was happening. While he and Caldwell had been talking, Salvadora's group had gone to ground and were no longer visible.

Up on the rise, the men were scurrying around while moving towards lower ground. Then Lincoln noticed two women on the crest of the rise using their elevated position to shoot at the men below.

'The women didn't walk into a trap,' Caldwell said with admiration in his tone. 'They were staying in the open as bait and it's the men who walked into their trap.'

'Perhaps we've both underestimated Salvadora,' Lincoln said as he got to his feet.

As gunfire rattled away, he moved on quickly. Caldwell slipped in beside him and with their heads down they ran towards the rise.

With them being more reckless in their approach Lincoln reckoned they'd reach the gunfight within a minute, but the chances of them being able to help anyone diminished by the moment. First one man and then another cried out and then went tumbling down the slope as the women at the top cut through their ranks.

The remaining two men panicked and ran out from their covered positions. They hurried around the rise before heading to ground level, after which they ran towards Lincoln and Caldwell.

The two women fired at them and gunfire peppered at their heels forcing them to speed up, and that encouraged the larger group of women to show themselves. They emerged from hiding, coming up in a more spread out formation than the one they had been in when Lincoln had last seen them.

Shots whistled out around the fleeing men, and with the situation looking desperate for them, several men slipped out from El Dorado with guns brandished. They didn't get far.

Even before they could reach a defensive position of a boulder a dozen yards away, lead hammered into the ground around them forcing them to beat a hasty retreat.

'Over here,' Lincoln shouted, waving the two fleeing men on.

He directed a stern look at Caldwell, but Caldwell showed no sign that he would argue as he slid to a halt and then dropped down on his haunches. A moment later lead whistled over Lincoln's head.

He couldn't see who had fired and he reckoned the shot hadn't been aimed at him, but he joined Caldwell in lowering himself into the scrub. Then, on hands and feet, he scurried along seeking to emerge in a different position.

He covered ten yards before the shooting resumed. Then a cry of pain sounded around fifty feet away. When he drew himself higher it was to see that one of the women had been hit for the first time.

The injury had been only a glancing wound to her upper arm, but this first setback had ensured that the other women were peering around in concern. Then Lincoln saw why they were worried.

Domingo's men may not have been aware of

Salvadora's trap, but Salvadora hadn't anticipated the full extent of Domingo's plans. Twenty yards away two men, including a man who matched the description Lincoln had been given of Domingo, were lying in a small depression waiting for the women to come towards them.

The two fleeing men scurried on to join them, where they quickly spread out along the lip of the depression. While they raised their guns to await the first woman's approach, Lincoln kicked at the ground in frustration, fearing that his slim chance of stopping the situation from escalating out of control had just become even slimmer.

When Caldwell shuffled along to join Lincoln, he considered the scene and then frowned.

'This looks bad,' he said.

'It does,' Lincoln said. 'So we have to work together if we're going to stop this situation getting worse.'

'Sure.' Caldwell smiled. Then, without warning, he jumped to his feet and started firing at Domingo's men.

He hammered a shot into the back of the man furthest to the right making him go sprawling against the lip of the depression before he went sliding down to the bottom on his chest. Then Caldwell moved his gun to the left to aim at the next man.

Lincoln lunged for Caldwell's gun arm, but he wasn't quick enough to stop him firing again. Caldwell's next target had been turning round and so the lead sliced into the man's side, dropping him.

'That isn't the way to calm this situation,' Lincoln muttered as he dragged Caldwell down to his knees in the scrub.

'I'm just doing what I should have done on the day Domingo Villaruel first rode into my town.'

Lincoln shook his head and with a snarl Caldwell launched a backhanded blow at Lincoln's face. Lincoln raised his forearm to parry the blow and then jerked forward with his hands raised aiming to bundle Caldwell to the ground.

Caldwell resisted and the two men rocked from side to side. As they strained for supremacy, consternation erupted in the depression.

From the corner of his eye Lincoln saw that the gunfire from behind had made one of the men panic and he was scrambling up to ground level on hands on knees. When he gained his feet he ran on for two paces before the advancing women fired at him.

The women were yet to emerge from the scrub and come into Lincoln's sight, but he saw the man flinch back as a gunshot slammed into his upper chest. With defiance the man fired at the women.

He got in two shots before a prolonged burst of lead sliced into his chest and he tipped over to drop from view. The women whooped in delight and Salvadora raised herself to shout a taunt.

Then Lincoln had other matters to worry about when Caldwell pressed forward and knocked him over on to his back. Caldwell pinned down Lincoln's left arm with his gun hand then moved for his right arm.

Lincoln had no intention of shooting his fellow lawman and he jerked his gun away from Caldwell with an obvious gesture, but Caldwell still grabbed his upper arm and then settled his weight down on him. Lincoln pressed his elbow back on the ground for leverage and with his anger at Caldwell's behaviour growing he flexed his arm as he prepared to dash his gun against the side of Caldwell's head.

Then a shadow spread across the scrub a moment before Domingo came running into view. He was hurrying along with his head down, clearly not having expected to come across two men. His eyes were wide and staring, his experiences of being on the receiving end of trouble having taken its toll.

When Domingo saw the two lawmen he skidded to a halt and then swung up his gun to shoot them. Lincoln moved quicker than Domingo, however, and he jerked his gun to the side and fired, but with Caldwell holding his arm the shot flew wide giving Domingo enough time to fire.

Domingo's gunshot sliced into the ground a few inches from Lincoln's face kicking dirt across his cheek and this action appeared to make Caldwell come to his senses. He released Lincoln's arm and so, unencumbered, Lincoln fired again.

This time his shot caught Domingo in the stomach making him double over. Domingo stumbled forward for a pace and struggled to raise his gun, but before Lincoln could fire again, a gunshot thundered into Domingo's back from behind as one of the women got him in her sights.

Domingo stood up straight and then staggered backwards until he tumbled into the depression. When he disappeared from view, Lincoln turned to Caldwell.

'With the leader shot up, we have to join forces to keep the peace,' he said.

Caldwell didn't meet Lincoln's eye, but he slapped the marshal on the shoulder and then started to get off him. With Caldwell's apparent acquiescence Lincoln twisted round and scrambled out from under him, but then a sickening thud slammed into the back of his head.

The next Lincoln knew he was lying on his chest with his nose pressed into the dirt and another round of gunfire reports were tearing out.

The noises sounded as if they were a great distance away. Then his vision darkened.

'I reckon Salvadora's going to win,' Murphy said with surprise.

'And she sure doesn't need our help,' Buster said.

Murphy and Buster were now lying on their chests on the edge of the rocky area that surrounded El Dorado. Letisha had stayed with them after untying their bonds and although she had urged them to stay quiet, they had been able to work out Salvadora's plan.

She had approached El Dorado in a way that looked cautious enough to appear as if she was planning a sneak attack, but which had also not been cautious enough to avoid being spotted. So Domingo had sent out two groups to attack the women, leading one group himself, but her actions had been a clever subterfuge and it was the men who had been cut down.

Now the wounded Domingo had been dragged back to lie close to El Dorado while the women moved forward. The leader was still alive – presumably Salvadora wanted him to witness the final demise of his empire – but he was so badly injured he could barely raise his head.

The women were approaching the easier route down into the depression while Letisha watched the path out at the other end.

Murphy had caught sight of another woman lying close by and guarding the near side of the depression. So he had no doubt that Salvadora had effectively trapped everyone who was still loyal to Domingo.

Even though Salvadora clearly knew what she was doing, he didn't like the thought of not having a weapon to hand. As Salvadora gestured and two women fired at the lip of the depression, he looked around for inspiration and to his surprise he saw someone approaching them.

This person was keeping low and using the available cover in the undulating ground, but Murphy could see enough to note it was a man. He got Letisha's attention and pointed.

Letisha glanced at the man, but a few moments later Salvadora's group moved towards the lip of the depression forcing her to dart her gaze back and forth, torn between which danger to concentrate on. So Murphy moved towards the approaching man.

He walked upright, no longer trying to stay hidden, figuring that his best chance was to approach his target quickly and overcome him. The man kept his head down as he continued his stealthy approach and so Murphy got to within ten paces of him before he was heard.

As the man jerked his head up to look at him, Murphy broke into a run, but then in a shocking moment he recognized the unexpected newcomer. He dug in a heel and slid to a halt.

'Sheriff Caldwell!' he gasped.

'Sure am,' Caldwell said.

Then, with the need for stealth gone, the sheriff stood upright and advanced on Murphy, who stood paralyzed by surprise until Caldwell grabbed his arm and marched him on towards the others.

Letisha turned to watch them approach, displaying the same emotions that Murphy reckoned he was showing; first concern and then surprise. For his part Buster edged away clearly torn between running and seeing how this fraught situation would play out.

'You're too late to stop this,' Letisha said.

'I didn't come here to make you women suffer,' Caldwell said.

He stopped and shoved Murphy away brusquely making him stumble to his knees. Then he directed glares at both him and Buster confirming who he did want to make suffer.

Letisha cautiously raised herself and then moved back for a pace so she could watch both Caldwell and the developing gun battle.

'Whatever your reasoning, stay out of this,' she said.

Caldwell conceded her demand with a shrug and stood over Murphy, who struggled to work out how he should react and so settled for keeping his head down. Buster continued to move away from Caldwell and so the sheriff drew his gun and directed him to join Murphy.

Then there was nothing left for Murphy and Buster to do other but to watch the assault on El Dorado.

Salvadora had spread her forces out around one end of the lip of the depression and while laying down covering gunfire the women moved closer so that they could see more of the scene below.

Murphy expected the men to retreat under the overhang and force the women to go down to flush them out, but as it turned out Sigmund Gaunt led four men out of El Dorado. They ran, but with the last few yards back to ground level being steep, their pace was slow and two men were cut down before they could fire a single shot.

Sigmund had picked out Salvadora's location accurately and he charged towards her, shooting on the run. Two shots hammered into the ground around her before she fired at him, hitting him in the side.

While roaring his defiance Sigmund ran on for another two paces until Salvadora's second shot hit him in the stomach. He stumbled on for another pace before his legs buckled and he dropped to his knees.

He swayed and then raised a knee as he tried to stand, but he failed to gain his feet. Then he keeled over on to his chest.

Sigmund's demise made the other two men lose heart. They skidded to a halt and then backtracked to the depression, but with ruthless efficiency gunfire peppered into them from both sides.

The moment the men collapsed, three women hurried to the edge of the depression. At first they kept low while craning their necks as they considered the scene cautiously, but then they provided firm nods and stood upright suggesting the battle might have already been won.

Salvadora moved over to Domingo and tapped his side with her boot. He flinched away from the light blow, but Salvadora nodded approvingly, confirming she had hoped to capture him alive.

She beckoned another woman to stand guard over him and then ordered the other women to take up positions around the edge of the depression. Then she moved on purposefully towards the other end.

'So you were shooting in the scrub,' she said, glaring at the sheriff. 'What are you doing here?'

'I came for these two,' Caldwell said.

'I didn't mean that.' Salvadora swung to a halt before him. 'I warned you to stay where you were.'

'I'm a lawman. I don't take orders from someone who took me prisoner.'

'And now you intend to take these men prisoner?'

132

Caldwell nodded at Buster. Then he opened his mouth to explain, but before he could speak Salvadora used the distraction to swing her gun round and fire a quick shot that sliced into the sheriff's side.

Caldwell went down on one knee, his expression a mixture of pain and surprise. A second shot to the chest downed him, leaving Letisha to be the one looking at Salvadora with surprise.

'You shot a lawman,' she said. 'You've just condemned us all.'

'I warned that lawman to stay away,' Salvadora said without concern. 'There can be no witnesses to what happens here today.'

Letisha frowned and looked towards El Dorado, but then she winced a moment before Murphy picked up on the inference. By then it was too late to act as Salvadora turned her gun on Letisha.

'The battle is over,' Letisha said. 'I don't reckon the rest of the men will give us any trouble.'

'I'll make sure no man ever troubles us again.' Salvadora shot a sneering glance at Murphy and Buster before glaring at Letisha. 'So that still leaves you to decide if you're with me or not.'

CHAPTER 14

'You'll never get away with this,' Lincoln murmured groggily.

'He didn't,' Mary replied while shaking his shoulder.

Lincoln groaned and forced himself up to a sitting position. This action proved to be unwise as his vision swayed and his head throbbed, making him groan some more.

When he'd fought off his confusion, he saw that Caldwell had gone, and that it was Mary and Chastity who had roused him. He accepted he'd been knocked out for a while and so gingerly he got to his feet to look towards El Dorado.

Everything was quiet there, but the women's sombre expressions suggested this wasn't good news.

'What happened?' Lincoln said as he fingered his scalp gingerly.

'Domingo's men took on Salvadora,' Mary said. 'They lost.'

Mary glanced at Chastity, who lowered her head.

'We reckon she killed Sheriff Caldwell,' Chastity said. 'Then she headed down into El Dorado. Based on what she did to the prospectors we were with, I don't reckon she'll leave anyone alive to tell the tale.'

Lincoln winced as he located a lump and then turned back to the women.

'How long ago did this happen?'

'Not long.' Chastity shrugged. 'We waited until the shooting stopped and then moved closer to El Dorado, but when we found Caldwell's body we backed away before she saw us.'

'Then we still have time to do something.'

'But what can we do?' Chastity shrugged. 'All the women are determined to follow Salvadora no matter what she asks them to do.'

'Except us,' Mary said, making Chastity nod.

Lincoln didn't have an answer. So while he considered the two women, he stretched and took deep breaths to fight away the nausea-inducing headache that threatened to ensure he'd be in no fit state to do anything.

Mary was more confident than Chastity, although Chastity was more thoughtful and possibly more competent, but even so, by seeking their help he would endanger their lives. He shook his head, dismissing the thought, and that made a bolt of pain slice through his head.

He must have registered his distress as Chastity hurried to their pile of discarded belongings and returned with water. She signified that Lincoln should kneel down and while he drank his fill she fussed over the bump on his head before settling for pressing a wet kerchief over it.

Her ministrations reduced his discomfort and gave him time to think. So when she removed the kerchief he stood up and signified that they should join him in moving on to El Dorado.

'Before we make any hasty plans we have to find out what's happening now,' he said. 'But in case Salvadora is going further than just taking revenge on Domingo, tell me who else might be having reservations.'

'Letisha,' Mary and Chastity said together before Chastity silenced and signified that Mary should continue. 'She's the only one to openly oppose Salvadora. The other women listen to her, or at least they do until Salvadora cuts her down.'

'In that case while I cut Salvadora down, I may need your help in getting a message to Letisha.'

Both women nodded, but they said nothing more as they moved closer to the depression. When they reached a length of rock at the edge, Lincoln ran his gaze over the bodies that had been left where they'd fallen until Mary pointed out which one was Caldwell's.

The sheriff was lying apart from the other bodies and so Lincoln presumed that despite knocking him out he had still tried to do his duty and that had led him to defy Salvadora.

He fingered the back of his head, finding that it was less sore than before. Then, with the women shuffling along behind him, he moved on cautiously.

When he could see down into the depression, he discovered that he wasn't yet too late. Around twenty prospectors were standing in the middle of El Dorado while the women stood at regular intervals around them.

Salvadora was at one end conferring with two other women. They were standing over Domingo's hunched-over form.

Their agitated demeanours suggested they didn't have a firm plan yet. Lincoln peered at each of the women, but he couldn't see Letisha.

When Mary and Chastity joined him they pointed her out, and the sight made all three of them wince before they dropped down to ensure they weren't seen. Letisha was standing with Murphy and Buster in the centre of the depression.

'At least Murphy is still alive,' Chastity said, patting Mary's arm. 'That means we can still do something.'

'Without Letisha's help, what can we do?' Mary said.

They both looked at Lincoln, who provided the most confident smile he could muster.

'It looks bad, but it could be worse,' he said. 'As Letisha is being held prisoner, we know she'll help us if she can, and we have a dependable deputy and perhaps a wronged man down there, too.'

Mary firmed her jaw. 'We'll find a way to get a message down to her.'

Lincoln nodded and then raised himself, and he found that during their short discussion Salvadora had made a decision. She was gesturing at the guarding women and they were herding their captives towards one side of the depression.

'We saw an overhang and several caves below us,' Chastity said.

'That's good news,' Lincoln said. 'Hopefully Salvadora has decided against killing the men straight away and will keep them captive while she decides what to do next.'

Lincoln then had to wince when he found what Salvadora's next move would be. The two women she had conferred with headed for the slope that led out of the depression.

Within a minute these women would emerge on to flat ground and then they couldn't fail to spot him.

'Just do what she says and don't give her cause to do anything rash,' Letisha said, pulling Buster along to join her in heading to the cave.

Buster moved on, but Murphy dallied until one of the guards gestured at him with a gun. Murphy glared at her before he hurried on to join Letisha.

'Salvadora has already gone too far,' he said. 'She shot up Sheriff Caldwell.'

Letisha frowned and as the first men were herded

into the cave she slowed to a halt. She turned to face the nearest guard.

'I need to talk to Salvadora.' Letisha sighed. 'I've made my decision and I'm with her.'

As the guard moved away, Letisha glanced at Buster from the corner of her eye and then at the cave. Getting the hint, Buster moved on and Murphy followed, but both men stopped a few yards in from the entrance where they could watch what Letisha did next.

'Do you reckon Letisha can calm Salvadora down?' Murphy asked when the guard had gathered Salvadora's attention.

'I reckon so,' Buster said. 'Letisha just needs to make her see that she's eliminated her enemies and now that she's had her revenge she should move on.'

Murphy glanced over his shoulder at the huddled mass of prospectors, seeing only fear and tiredness in their eyes.

'I don't reckon any of these men sided with Domingo.'

'They just wanted his protection.' Buster edged closer to Murphy, and with Salvadora now joining Letisha, he lowered his voice. 'But what about Lincoln? If Caldwell found this place, it's possible Lincoln will, too.'

Bearing in mind the two lawmen's antipathy Murphy wasn't sure they would be together, but as he watched Letisha and Salvadora talk, the mention of

Lincoln made him recall the marshal's last advice to him.

Following his instincts had made him free Buster and that had led him to El Dorado. So he wondered what his instincts would tell him to do now.

No ideas would come, but when he saw that Salvadora was waving a dismissive hand at Letisha, he figured a lawman should try to seize control of this situation. He took a decisive step forward, but Buster must have worked out his intent as he grabbed his shoulder and drew him away from the entrance.

'I'm a lawman,' Murphy said. 'I have to do something.'

'Sometimes doing nothing is the most sensible option,' Buster said. 'Trust Letisha and don't rile Salvadora.'

Murphy struggled, but Buster had gathered a firm grip and so he relented.

'All right, but at the first sign that Letisha isn't having an effect, I do something.'

Buster winked. 'If that happens, we'll both do something.'

With that decision made they moved deeper into the cave. Murphy considered the two intact crates that were still lying where they'd opened them the night before.

He tipped them over, making one of the lids break in two. Buster helped him and in moments they both had a short plank they could wield as a cudgel.

Murphy accepted that these weapons were poor

when faced with a dozen guns, but he felt more confident holding something in his hand. Their efforts attracted the other men's attention and so Murphy moved around them to see if anyone had any weaponry.

The men had been searched, but several had held on to small knives and other metal utensils. With these discoveries encouraging everyone, Murphy was pleased to see some of their fear recede and so when Salvadora came into the cave entrance, everyone swung round to face her in a determined manner.

'How much longer are you keeping us in here?' one man demanded.

'When are you leaving?' another man asked.

Then the questions came quickly and even rumbled on when Salvadora raised a hand calling for calm. Accordingly, she beckoned and two women stepped up to flank her.

As the questions petered out Murphy and Buster moved to one side letting them see that Letisha was walking away from the cave while Domingo was being dragged forward. Domingo's head was held low and he barely reacted when he was thrown to the ground beside the pile of wood he had built that morning.

'All will be decided now,' Salvadora said when she had quiet. 'My quarrel is with Domingo Villaruel and those who sided with him.'

'That man was a piece of scum,' someone said, making others murmur in support.

'I'm pleased to hear you say that. Now we'll find out

141

if you believe it.' She turned to one side to point at Domingo. 'I intend to kill him for what he did to us. Then I'll leave. But if anyone comes out to help him, I'll shoot them.'

She cast her measured gaze around the cave and when nobody spoke she walked away to stand over Domingo. She waited, perhaps hoping Domingo would react, but the man lay still, seemingly beyond being able to retort.

She walked off leaving the other two women to deal with Domingo. Most of the men in the cave turned away, but Buster edged closer to Murphy.

'Those lawman instincts of yours aren't telling you to do something stupid, are they?' he asked.

Murphy sighed. 'They are.'

'Domingo is barely alive. Even if you saved him, he wouldn't survive for long enough to get back to Russell Creek, and even then, after everything he's done he'll—'

'I'm not thinking about him. I don't trust Salvadora.'

He looked around for others who might be looking concerned, but Salvadora's promise had placated most people. He turned back to Buster, who was looking at the entrance with his eyes wide.

Murphy followed his gaze and winced. Salvadora had completed Domingo's intent from that morning and one of the women was lighting the pile of wood while the other woman dragged Domingo closer to it.

'She means to burn him to death,' Buster murmured.

'While smoking us all out of here in the process.'

'And if anyone comes out, she'll deem them to be trying to help Domingo and she'll kill them.'

CHAPTER 15

Mary and Chastity walked openly towards the two approaching women. They were greeted warmly, and so Lincoln snaked backwards along the rock.

The best cover he could find was available beyond the end of the stretch of rock where he was able to lie down on his chest in the dirt. He faced the depression and watched the women.

Mary gestured in the opposite direction to Lincoln before she and Chastity moved down into the depression and that had the intended effect when the other women took up positions looking that way. Lincoln watched them while willing them to move further away so that he could see what was happening in El Dorado.

Mary and Chastity had left with no clear plan worked out as to how they would gather Letisha's support. Despite this, Lincoln still hoped he could end this situation without further violence.

That hope receded when a tendril of smoke drifted up out of the depression. The guards swirled round to look down, their sudden reactions suggesting the fire hadn't been planned.

With a growing feeling that this development was a bad one, Lincoln shuffled forward. At first he moved slowly, but then someone shouted in alarm, a sound which was followed by a sustained burst of demands.

The cries came to his left, which was where the guards were looking. One woman even put her hand to her mouth in a show of being shocked and so Lincoln speeded up.

He scrambled across the ground, the thickness of the smoke and the cries of alarm growing by the moment. With him being more reckless, the guards flinched and swung round to face him, but Lincoln put them from his mind and moved on until he reached the lip of the depression.

At first, he struggled to see where the smoke was coming from as the plumes were drifting over the edge and masking his view of the scene below, but he could see Letisha standing with Mary and Chastity. The reaction of the two guards made them look his way and they gestured frantically at the corner of the depression.

Lincoln didn't know what was concerning them, but the fact that he couldn't see the captives made him fear the worst. As he sought a gap in the smoke to let him see more, the guards raised their guns and blasted off a round apiece at him.

The shots were high and presumably meant to warn him off, but they gathered the attention of several women below, who scurried into view. Salvadora was amongst them, and his arrival couldn't have been a surprise as she gestured for several women to move to higher ground while shooing the others away.

When this latter group moved out of sight towards the source of the smoke, Lincoln accepted that the fire had sinister intent. He needed to act quickly, but several women were already clambering out of the depression on one side while the first two were moving purposefully around the opposite edge towards him.

With them seeking to trap him from either side, he looked for an alternative route down. His gaze alighted on a pole set against the rock below him.

He craned his neck over the side and saw that the pole supported one end of a barrier that covered half of an overhang below him. The top of the pole was two feet below and the top of the barrier another foot below that, so in a sudden decision he swung round and lowered his legs over the side.

With his feet dangling he kicked to either side until he'd trapped the pole between his ankles. Then, having orientated himself, he placed his elbows on firm ground and lowered himself.

The top of the barrier turned out to be further away than he'd thought it would be and he rooted around with his boots in increasing frustration as he struggled to locate it. His movements made his elbows slip and he slid down, forcing him to plant both hands on to the rock to still himself.

For a frozen moment he dangled, suspended over

the side with his boots dragging across the rock as he struggled to work out if he was inches or feet away from his target. Then the women moving in on him from either side started firing and this time they didn't use warning shots.

Lead sliced into the rock on either side of him kicking rock shards against his arms and making him flinch. He lost his grip and he dropped, but only for a few inches, as with a lurch his feet clattered down on the top of the barrier.

He glanced down and confirmed his feet were resting on a firm base. But with his chin level with the lip of the depression, he reckoned he'd committed himself as he would struggle to get back up.

With one hand pressed to the rock and the other gripping the pole he bent down until he was kneeling on the wood. Then he looked for the next place to reach, but the smoke was becoming thicker, watering his eyes and making him cough.

Worse, gunfire rattled below. None of it hit the rock around him, although several men shouted. One of the voices was Murphy's and he was demanding some-thing, but in response a volley of gunshots tore out.

In desperation Lincoln grabbed the pole with two hands and planted a foot against the rock on either side. With his body hunched over, he clambered down.

At first, he dragged his feet down slowly, but after a few manoeuvres he gained in confidence. He tried a larger movement, but then his foot jerked forward alarmingly.

Once he'd overcome his shock, he figured he'd reached the top of the overhang faster than he'd expected, but that conclusion didn't help him as he floundered. He settled for wrapping his arms around the pole, and then resumed working his way down.

A crack sounded below and desperate cries went up making him stop and look around. The smoke was too dense for him to see anything other than the top of the overhang, but strangely, he didn't have to look upwards to see it as it was directly in front of him.

Then, in a disorientating moment, he worked out what he was seeing. In shock he looked to the left.

All along the overhang the barrier was peeling away from its supports as it toppled over. The pole that Lincoln was climbing down was already skewed at an angle and as more cracks sounded it continued to tip over.

Lincoln was still thirty feet off the ground, so he did the only thing he could do and held on to the pole. When the barrier lost its battle to stay upright and toppled, he swung round the pole to put his back to the overhang.

This direction let him face the depression. Beneath him, the women were scurrying to flee the barrier before it hit the ground while the downdraft from the falling structure wafted away some of the smoke and revealed that the fire was set before a cave.

Lincoln had other matters to worry about when the pole angled down sharply. He mentally rehearsed his next actions, deciding he would brace himself just before the pole hit the ground and then roll forward.

He reckoned he could emerge from the crash relatively unscathed. Then, with a shudder, the pole cracked and the top half sprang forward.

Lincoln lost his grip of the pole and had the unsettling feeling of flying forward before he slammed down to the ground amidst the debris from the barrier.

His vision swirled around him as he rolled and even when he thudded to a halt on his back it still continued to swirl. With disorientated and weak movements he tried to force himself up to a sitting position, but his limbs refused to obey him.

With his head pounding and a dull buzzing in his ears, he flopped back down. Shouts of consternation rose up, but they appeared to be some distance away and in his disorientated state they didn't feel as if they should concern him.

Then Salvadora loomed up over him, and she was smiling.

Lincoln willed himself to concentrate. Then, with a sudden movement, he rooted around for his gun, but she planted a firm foot on his wrist, pinning it to the ground.

'That was almost a spectacular entrance,' she said.

She reached down and claimed Lincoln's gun. Then she stepped back and tossed the gun aside giving Lincoln room to double over and then force himself up to a kneeling position.

This time he managed to move and aside from a

battered feeling, he reckoned he'd come to earth in an intact state, although he couldn't say the same for the barrier. Heaps of wood and poles stuck up along the length of the overhang with the far end having come down beside the fire, which was now licking at the edge of the debris.

Behind the fire the captives were moving around in a cave entrance. The guards held guns on them while casting glances from them to Salvadora and back again in an obvious sign that they were awaiting instructions.

'This ends now,' Lincoln said. 'Let the captives get away from the fire and then lay down your arms. I'll deal with the situation from here.'

Salvadora shook her head. 'I warned you to stay away and to let me deal with Domingo.'

She looked towards the fire in a pointed manner inviting Lincoln to follow her gaze and this let him see Domingo's form lying close to the spreading fire.

'You're planning to burn Domingo alive?'

'There's not much life left in him, but I'm sure he's regretting what he did to me and the other women.'

'You suffered, but delivering justice is a serious duty and not something anyone does cruelly.'

'You won't judge me and nobody will help him.' She raised her voice and her final words echoed around El Dorado making the guards move towards the cave. 'Not you, not any man.'

Lincoln judged that the fire was spreading away from Domingo and so he didn't have to act quickly, but with the smoke growing denser the captives sought to edge past the fire.

They moved for only a few paces before one of the women fired. Her shot was over the captives' heads and so they still advanced, but when another woman joined her in shooting, most of the men hurried back into the cave entrance.

Two men didn't join them in retreating. They were carrying short planks, but the smoke shrouded their forms.

They advanced several cautious paces and when the smoke parted briefly Lincoln saw that they were Murphy and Buster. They looked at him, immediately realizing that his unexpected arrival gave them their best chance, but also clearly being unable to work out how to use it with so many guns being held on them.

'I don't intend to help anyone,' Lincoln said. He steadied himself and got to his feet. 'I'm delivering justice.'

Salvadora nodded. 'I'd hoped you'd force my hand and make this easier for me.'

She raised her gun and in so doing Lincoln noted where she'd thrown his gun. It lay five paces away and to her side, which was too far for him to reach and so he considered Salvadora, wondering what he could say to buy him a few more moments.

He saw no hope that she would back down as she sighted his chest and so he looked past her seeking out Mary and Chastity. These women had joined Letisha and they were unarmed, but strangely they weren't watching his confrontation with Salvadora.

He must have conveyed his surprise as Salvadora half-turned to look at what had concerned him. Like Lincoln, she noted they were looking to the top of the depression, but whatever was holding their attention was hidden behind smoke.

Their reactions made the other women turn and Murphy and Buster took advantage by edging along towards the nearest guard.

Most of the women moved their heads to the side showing they were watching someone approach, making Lincoln hope that help had arrived, but he groaned when he caught his first sight of what was holding their interest.

Only one man had arrived. He was walking slowly along the lip of the depression, his form moving in and out of patches of smoke and making it hard for Lincoln to identify him.

When the man reached a path down into El Dorado he stopped and considered the scene until he faced Chastity. She put a hand to her mouth, confirming who the newcomer was.

Joshua Vincent had finally arrived in El Dorado.

CHAPTER 16

With everyone watching him, Joshua walked down the side of the depression and then across the base.

His gait was unsteady and when he drew closer, Lincoln could see his stooped form and haggard expression suggesting that since he'd left them the night before, he had walked under the hot sun without sustenance.

Joshua stopped before the group of three women where Chastity took a pace forward. The other two women flanked her, seemingly aware of the likely danger, although they wouldn't know of Joshua's promise.

'For forty days and forty nights our saviour walked through a wilderness not unlike like this one,' Joshua announced, his voice clear throughout El Dorado. 'I'm not blessed with such fortitude, but I have also sought an answer to what I must do.'

'What is that answer?' Chastity asked.

'I've decided that I must forgive you and I will lead

you from this place.' He looked around. 'I will lead you all from this place.'

Chastity gasped and then dropped to her knees in relief, which made Joshua move forward and place a comforting hand on his daughter's shoulder. Then he turned to consider the other women.

For long moments nobody moved. Then one of the guards broke the impasse by throwing her gun to the ground.

'No!' Salvadora shouted. 'Don't listen to that man. He never had an answer to our problems.'

She swung her gun away from Lincoln to aim it at the surrendered woman, but this action had the opposite effect to what Salvadora intended when another woman threw down her weapon.

Salvadora swirled around as she looked for support, and so Lincoln took a short pace towards his discarded gun while at the cave Murphy shuffled towards the nearest guard.

With the confrontation about to come to a head, Lincoln settled his weight on his toes. Then he took a long pace and leapt for his gun.

He gathered the weapon up and rolled. Then, lying on his side, he jerked the gun up to aim at Salvadora, but he stilled his arm when he saw that she'd directed her attention and her gun back on to him.

'Your women are now seeing sense,' he said. 'It's time to prove what kind of leader you are.'

'It sure is,' Salvadora said.

She sneered, seemingly preparing to fire, but then

she flinched, a gunshot sounding a moment later as blood trickled out through a rip on her sleeve. Lincoln couldn't see who had turned against her. Salvadora glanced around, seemingly unable to work it out either.

She put a hand to her wounded gun arm as she backed away, but she didn't take her gun away from Lincoln.

'I reckon you're no longer leading these women,' Lincoln said, inching his gun up. 'They've found a better way.'

'Follow me,' she shouted. 'You will all follow me, not that man.'

From the corner of his eye Lincoln saw other women throw down their weapons, a sight that made Salvadora flare her eyes. Then, with a hand pressed tightly to her wound, she sighted Lincoln down the barrel of the gun.

In retaliation Lincoln snapped up his arm, but before he could shoot gunfire tore out. It took him a moment to identify that he'd heard two shots and another moment to notice that Salvadora hadn't fired.

Then she keeled over with blood oozing from her side. Lincoln jumped to his feet and noted that the guards had thrown down their guns while the captives were streaming out of the cave and away from the fire.

Once he'd confirmed the situation was under control, he looked for who had fired. He saw two scenarios.

Murphy had seized a gun from one of the guards,

and Letisha had claimed a gun from another woman. Murphy looked shocked, while Letisha was nodding with approval.

Lincoln nodded to her and then moved over to Salvadora.

'I'm sorry it had to end this way,' he said, standing over her.

'Domingo?' she murmured with her voice barely audible and her eyes closed.

Lincoln looked at the fire and although he wasn't sure, he knelt down and replied using a kindly voice.

'He's dead,' he said.

Salvadora gasped in relief, but once she'd exhaled, she didn't breathe in again. Lincoln knelt beside her as the other women gravitated towards them.

They formed a circle, and for a while nobody spoke.

Salvadora lay still and the fire crackled, but when the wind changed direction and wafted smoke their way, everyone moved away.

Lincoln joined Murphy, who still sported a shocked expression.

'Don't think ill of her,' Murphy said.

'I don't,' Lincoln said. 'I pity her, but I think ill of what she did, and I'm obliged for what you did.'

Murphy tipped back his hat. 'I sure don't feel good about killing a woman, and one who had suffered at that.'

'I'm not sure it was you. Both you and Letisha shot at her, but even if your bullet hit her, you acted against someone who was in the wrong to save others, which is what a good lawman should do.'

This revelation appeared to help Murphy as he mustered a nod, but his concerned expression showed he would still need time to reconcile his actions in his own mind. Lincoln gave him that time by going to check on the others.

Domingo Villaruel was dead, although he looked as if he had been dead for a while, having succumbed to his injuries before he could be dragged into the fire.

The other prospectors were all uninjured and no matter what role they had played in creating the situation, the disgusted looks they shot at Domingo's body convinced Lincoln that he should take no further action against them.

He concluded the same for the women. Now that Salvadora had been killed, they looked relieved and from what Lincoln had seen, their activities had been carried out by Salvadora or at her behest.

Even better, the women gathered around Joshua as he offered them more words of wisdom, and belying what Caldwell had told him about their attitude to him they looked eager to listen to his message. While he spoke, Letisha came over to Lincoln.

'The women know they went too far,' she said, 'but they want to return to Russell Creek to ensure the full story is known.'

Lincoln looked at Murphy, who was standing with hunched shoulders, but when he saw that Lincoln was looking at him, he directed a firm nod at her.

'You're right,' Murphy said. 'We should all go back

to Russell Creek.'

Letisha smiled, but his comment made Buster raise his hands and take a cautious step backwards.

'After all I've been through,' Buster said, 'you can't make me go back there.'

'I reckon I can,' Murphy said. When Buster backed away for another pace, he raised a hand. 'But not as an escaped prisoner. I need you as a witness.'

Buster sighed with relief. 'I'm prepared to do that, but I'm still under arrest for killing Aaron Knight.'

'What we learned here proves you were justified in what you did.' Murphy glanced at Lincoln, and the marshal smiled approvingly. 'You may not have known that at the time, but I'm sure after thinking about it some more, you'll work things out in your own mind.'

'And I'll speak up for him,' Letisha said, stepping forward. 'As will all the women here. We've destroyed Domingo's operation in El Dorado, and you made a start in Russell Creek with Aaron, but there's still more of the guilty to root out back there.'

'Then the sooner we head back,' Buster said with a determined shake of a fist, 'the sooner we can end this forever.'

Murphy slapped him on the back, but then with a pensive expression he turned to Lincoln.

'Was that the right thing to do?' he asked.

'You're following your instincts and that's good enough for me.' Lincoln winked. 'But I wouldn't recommend that you make a habit of freeing your prisoners.'

'I'll remember that. Are you returning with us?'

Lincoln glanced around El Dorado, where already the prospectors were putting out the fire while others sought a way into the overhang to rescue their belongings. He shook his head.

'Nope. My work here is over and as your boss told me: what was happening in Russell Creek was no business of mine.'

Murphy shrugged. 'Except you ignored him.'

'I did.' Lincoln patted Murphy on the back. 'But that was only because I had no confidence in the law in Russell Creek.'

Lincoln waited while Murphy acknowledged his subtle compliment with a beaming smile. Then he turned away to search for the quickest path out of El Dorado.